Yorga On The Run

By Cliff Robison

Rock and Fire Press

Salinas, CA

Yorga On The Run

ISBN:
978-1-949005-24-0 (Print)
978-1-949005-25-7 (eBook)

Rock & Fire Press
Salinas, CA

N*I*A*C*IN denies any involvement.

Prologue:

SOUTH OF SALINAS, along highway 101, there are roughly 1200 people in a town with only three north-south streets. Two of those streets are named for presidents, and the third one might be.

An old Ford pickup, sun-faded two-tone green, with a home-made lumber rack stretching over the extended cab, was parked facing Northwest on Grant Street, the closest equivalent Chualar has to an actual main street. The middle-aged man who sat behind the wheel squinted up along the freeway, towards the setting sun as it filtered through the distant trees, and waited patiently.

A large square delivery truck, its blank white sides completely unmarked aside from some squiggly neon graffiti, lumbered over the freeway bridge and crossed in front of him, making its way towards Lincoln Street. It was mostly residential that way, but maybe they were going to the school. Delivering school lunches, maybe. Who knew?

Across the freeway, by the railroad tracks, some wooden crates were scattered on the ground. They lay among the thin stand of scraggly little eucalyptus trees between the train tracks and the nearest fields. They looked damaged, like maybe they had fallen off the train. Odd; normally freight is strapped down solidly.

But it wasn't Herb's problem, so he ignored it.

He raised a can of beer and sipped it slowly before putting it back between his knees. The sign on the shop window beside him advertised *cerveza barrata* – cheap beer. And it was even cold. Sort of. He thought about going back into the shop and getting some meat to grill outdoors that night, but he didn't want to take any chance on missing this meeting.

Two women came out of the bodega, talking as they pushed a small wire-mesh handcart. Two boys and a small girl followed them out, laughing and shouting in Spanish. The women paid no attention to the orbiting children, whose game seemingly involved tagging each other and then touching the handcart.

Herb turned his attention back to the freeway and took another sip of his beer.

Moments later, a once-white Crown Victoria, its quarter-panels lightly coated with a thin, tan layer of mud and dust, rolled up the off-ramp to a stop on the other side of the overpass. It looked like a police cruiser, but the spotlights were missing and there was no insignia on the doors. Herb watched as it crossed the narrow bridge over highway 101 and turned south onto Grant, then stopped across the street from his pickup truck.

The man who got out was a little overweight, but he was not someone who'd have trouble in a rowdy bar. He stood a bit above six feet, and his shoulders were broad. He was wearing slacks and a white shirt with a tie. His mustache ended sharply at the corners of his mouth, and had a straight edge along the vermilion border of his upper lip.

He looked both ways and then strolled casually over to the truck, leaning on his elbows just below the window. He nodded to the man behind the wheel.

"Herb, that's an open container," he said.

"Not your problem down here," snapped the older man. He took another sip of beer. "It's one beer and I'm what, two miles from my house?"

"Whatever."

"Honestly, Franz, you always gotta be a cop twenty-four seven?"

"Okay, forget I said anything. Why'd you call me down here?"

"Trying to save my pension," said Herb. He handed a small paper bag out the window. "What's that look like?"

"A blob of melted plastic," said Franz. "What's it from?" He offered the bag back to Herb, who waved it away.

"Remember that cannon you guys confiscated?"

"The Lahti, from that sniper?"

"Yeah, looked like a rifle, had a .80-caliber bore?"

"Okay, what about it?"

"That's the lower receiver."

"Pretty sure it's not. They didn't have plastics like this in 1939, and even if they did, they sure weren't making rifles out of it."

"That's what you sent me. I put that cannon up onto the workbench, I touched the torch to it, and the whole thing caught on fire. Smoke everywhere. That's what's left of the lower receiver."

"You would've known by the weight, before you torched it. Plastic would be too light."

Herb pointed to the bag. Franz pulled out the blob of plastic. It was permeated with tiny metal teardrop shapes.

"Dunno what that is," said Herb. "Looks like fishing weights, but when I hit 'em with the torch, I couldn't melt 'em. Couldn't even make 'em red."

"You're telling me…"

"That someone swapped all the important parts of that gun for pieces made of plastic, with metal in it for weight."

"That gun's been in evidence since the case."

"Until it got delivered to me for destruction. And that stuff stinks to high heaven. Cap yelled for hours about me smellin' up the shop with burnt plastic."

"Worse than the Limburger cheese sandwich thing?"

"I dunno what you got against Limburger."

"Smells like dirty socks, that's what I've got against it." He turned the plastic over in his hands. "So you're tellin' me somebody gave you a fake gun, and didn't think you'd notice."

"They probably think we smash 'em or something. Or put 'em in an incinerator. But we've gotta burn through the barrel and the chamber with a torch. Both of 'em have to be destroyed so you couldn't safely fix 'em. That's the law."

He sat up straighter and leaned forward so that he could look Franz in the eye. "Something stinks in that shop, and it's not plastic and it's not cheese. They keep tellin' me I can't count. Herb, we gave you ten guns, not six. Herb, you got the manifest wrong. Herb, the numbers don't match.

"I'm just an old farmer thinks he knows how to fix things. But I can count, and I know the paperwork says I melted more guns than I really melted. I make a ten, that zero turns into a six. I write one, it turns into seven. I told

Cap about it, but he says I'm crazy, and not to tell anyone cause they'll think I'm senile."

"They wouldn't think you were senile. Drunk, maybe, but not senile."

"Forget you. I'm serious, here."

"So you're showing me this because…"

"Because one day one of those guns I supposedly melted is gonna kill someone, and it's gonna come back on me. And then I go to jail, or I have a tragic accident at work. I don't like it either way." He emptied the beer can and dropped it in the passenger floor bed.

"I'm gonna need to talk to some people," said Franz. "I've got to document all this, bring my ell-tee in on it, start an investigation…"

"And it'll go in a big circle and bite my butt," said Herb. "If that's all you can do, forget I said anything. I don't want to have an accident at work. Except it's not an accident. Yeah, we never talked about this."

"I don't see a way to keep your name out of it."

"Okay, just forget about it. Forget I said anything at all." He started his engine and put the old truck into gear. Franz watched as it rolled to the intersection, turned right, and disappeared behind *Carniceria Los Quatro Hermanos*.

Detective Sergeant Franz Yorga stood in the street for a moment, holding the paper bag and the blob of plastic. Then he put the plastic into the bag and carried both to his trunk. He went a block south, made a u-turn, and then drove north on Grant until it merged into Highway 101.

Chapter One

ONE FINE OCTOBER day, at about eleven-fifteen, Detective Sergeant Franz Yorga threw a twenty onto the table of the little Sicilian restaurant on Gabilan Street, and walked out the door.

That was not surprising. He ate there often, and while the tip would be a bit excessive, it was not unusual for him to pay and leave before the check came. Such is the policeman's lot in life.

But instead of walking west to the police station on Lincoln Street, Yorga instead went north, past the Steinbeck Center. He crossed Salinas Street, and caught the light at Market just right.

When the Amtrak Coast Starlight thundered to a stop at the train station, Yorga was standing near the end of the platform, where the coach cars for Los Angeles would be. A white-shirted attendant opened the door and put down the yellow step so that two old ladies could disembark.

Yorga watched them for a moment as they tottered towards the station, wondering aloud if Dolores was going to meet them there. The attendant looked at Yorga.

"Didn't see any new passengers here on the manifest," he said.

"Ticket office is closed, but the sign says I can buy a ticket to Los Angeles on the train," said Yorga.

The car attendant frowned. He waved at a blue-shirted man coming out of the station. The man trotted over to them and nodded to the attendant.

"He wants a ticket to L.A.," said the attendant. "Says the ticket office is closed."

The conductor shrugged. "If she stepped away for a minute, she's back now," he said. "But you don't have time to go buy a ticket." He turned and pointed to the cars as if counting them, did some mental math, then turned back to Yorga.

"I've got five empties in Coach, but they're reserved from SLO south. I can put you in Business Class for seventy-three and change."

Yorga pulled some bills out of his pocket, but the conductor waved them away. "Wait till we're moving, and I'll come around for you. Meantime, go to the business car and pick a seat." He looked around. "No luggage? Did you check anything at the station?"

"Traveling light today," said Yorga. "Unplanned trip. No time to pack."

He stepped into the coach car, and the attendant picked up the step behind him. The door slammed and the train started, almost immediately. Yorga made his way up the narrow stairs, and then down the aisle, swaying slightly with the motion of the train.

Coach was nearly full, but Yorga kept going forward, through the doors at the front of each car. The third car he came to was only half full, and had leather seats, instead of cloth.

As he settled into a seat in business class, Yorga pulled a small folded paper from his coat pocket and glanced at it. It was written on a piece of scratch paper, about four inches on a side. The back had been part of a memo to City employees about a new parking plan. The paper had been folded, taped shut, and left for Yorga at the Sicilian café.

The message was simple, but very clear:

RUN LIKE HELL.

Chapter Two

BENTLEY WALKED INTO Lieutenant Jones'
office and waited for his superior to look up. Jones
finished typing something, hit the enter key with an air of
finality, and only then looked at Bentley.

"What can I do for you?"

"Seen Yorga?"

"Not my turn to keep track of him this week," said
Jones. "He's your partner."

"He didn't come back from lunch. He didn't say
anything to you about an appointment or anything?"

"You think he needs help?"

"I'm gonna go over to the Sicilian place and check it
out. See when he left."

"Call if you need back-up," said Jones. "Those
calzones are mighty big. Try the Hawaiian."

"A Sergeant goes missing and that's all you've got?"

"Close the door," said Jones. Bentley swung it to and looked back at Jones. "Between us, the less you ask about Yorga, the better you'll sleep nights. Clear?"

Bentley nodded.

"Leave the door open as you go," said Jones.

Bentley walked into the break room and drew a cup of Torino Blend from the oversized coffeemaker. It was a horrible brew. Bentley suspected that it consisted of the most badly burned beans from French and Italian blends, roasted a second time and then singed with a blowtorch before being bagged and sold. Whatever the method, it was beyond question that it produced a bitter and acidic cup of coffee-like liquid.

Bentley carried the oily solution back to his desk and perched it atop a stack of folders. He had found that leaving cups of coffee on his desk kept Jones from piling on more cases for him. With his desk duly booby-trapped, he slipped out the door.

Yorga sat in an armchair that was more expensive than opera seats, but lasted longer. The central coast slowly ebbed past. Train travel had two distinct advantages over airplanes, he decided. There was no security rigamarole getting on; that was the first thing. And there was a lot more room to stretch out. It was like a first class seat on a plane. He could put his feet up and recline his seat back without interfering with anyone else. In fact, there were only a dozen passengers, maybe, in the entire business-class car.

The disadvantage was that it took more time. A lot more time. But that really wasn't such a problem. He needed some time to think out his next move.

The note didn't come from Herb; he knew that. He also knew exactly why he was being told to run. The lid was off, and things were about to boil over.

So… The first question was whether he should warn Herb, but it was also moot. Herb didn't have a cell phone. If he called the Work Street yard and asked for Herb, someone would have to walk from the office to the shop, and then back to the welding bay. And they'd want to know who was calling. And then there'd be a record of the call.

Herb was probably already in custody, anyway.

Cell phones. Little GPS trackers. For a second, Yorga thought about putting his phone and the battery to it in separate trash receptacles somewhere on the train. But just having the battery out was good enough. The last place they could track him to would be the Sicilian café.

He'd need a new cell. On TV, they were called burners. When he got to LA, he'd buy a new one. Maybe two or three. He'd need cash so they couldn't track the purchase. And that raised another problem. His ATM card.

Okay, they'd know from the ATM transaction that he was in Los Angeles. Not necessarily a problem. Three-point-one million people in Los Angeles proper, and probably five or six times that in the surrounding cities. Or maybe a dozen times more, depending on how loosely you defined "surrounding." It would take a day, maybe two, to get a warrant to trace his debit card. So he'd get the cash in LA, and then he'd get out of town. There were lots of good places to hide in SoCal.

Once he had the new phone – the unregistered phone – he could check on the second question: How long before they raided his apartment? He figured he had probably a day till they got a warrant. They'd want him in custody first, so they could get enough on him to justify a warrant. And also to keep from walking in on him while he was cleaning his gun.

He'd have enough time to get a burner phone in LA. He might even be able to draw out enough cash to keep himself afloat for a while.

Fields were rolling by the window, green crops giving way to oil fields, then pastures and rolling hills. Paso Robles and Atascadero slid past. Yorga sighed. His world was on fire, and the most productive thing he could do at that moment would be to take a nap. He closed the curtain on his window, leaned the big soft chair back, and closed his eyes.

The call came in at two-oh-two. One eighty-seven, see patrol on-site. It was a little common-wall place in the North Salinas streets that are named for rivers in Spain. Bentley pulled up behind the two black-and-whites that were forming a chevron in the two-car driveway.

The front door was open. Bentley knew the patrolmen wouldn't have called him until the scene was secure, but he still had his right hand on his holster as he carefully stepped through the doorway. From cocked and locked, in his holster, he could put three rounds on target in under three seconds. So far, he hadn't ever had the need to. But there's always a first time.

The living room was dark. Beach towels with team logos hung over the curtain rods in place of blinds. The sliding glass door to the back yard was similarly darkened. A threadbare couch that looked like a Sally Ann discount special had seen way too much wear and tear, and maybe even a little bit of blood and fire. The thin gray carpet had permanent stains on the traffic paths.

"Police detective," he called out, as he stepped across the threshold into the living room.

"Back here!"

He headed towards the sound, through the living room, towards a ground floor bedroom. Two officers stood over the body of a man on the floor. His shirt was red with blood. A revolver lay next to his elbow.

One patrolman nodded towards the front room, and led Bentley out the front door. The other followed.

"So, yeah," said the patrolman. "We're just securing the scene till the coroner and the CSU get here. Not that it'll take much forensics. She was still standing there, pulling the trigger, when we got here." He nodded towards one of the black and whites.

Bentley glanced at the car, where a woman sat in the back seat. He assumed she was cuffed and had been read her rights.

"Domestic that got out of control?"

"That's pretty much what it looks like," said the second patrolman. "She's got a shiner and some bruises. Looks like a defensive cut on her forearm, plus some healed scars. She'll probably walk on the 187. Gonna be justified, looks like."

"Then she'll find some other guy to beat her up, and we'll get to repeat the whole thing in a couple years," said the first uniform. "They oughta have mandatory counseling in these things. How to pick guys you won't have to shoot."

"At least there's no kids," said the second uni.

"Listen," said Bentley, "That's all well and good for you to think stuff like that if you want to, but keep it to yourselves when the CSU and the coroner get here. We don't want any claims that we rushed to a conclusion. Just say what you saw, and keep the editorial comments off the record."

"Right, yeah, of course," said the first cop, "This is all just between us cops, you know? Nothing I'd want to be quoted on."

"These things can spiral," said the second officer, "Reminds me of the time a citizen found a bloody baseball bat on a sidewalk in the park. First cop on scene starts a door-to-door around the neighborhood, looking for a victim."

"Interesting," said Bentley. "I guess that could've been a blood-born pathogen on a path-born bludgeon."

"Yeah," said the first uniform, "But it turns out some kid got a nosebleed walking home from a game. Panicked, dropped his bat, ran home. EMTs confirmed it was heat-related or something."

"No foul after all," said Bentley.

"But it ran on the nightly six-o'clock news as a violent kidnapping. Took us two weeks to get the straight story out there."

"That guy down at the Gazette thought it was a cover-up," confirmed his partner. "You know that one columnist?"

"All the more reason to make sure you don't say anything you shouldn't about this," said Bentley. He glanced around for nosy neighbors and lookie-loos, but the street was quiet.

He turned as an additional car arrived. Lt. Jones came to a stop behind Bentley's unmarked Crown Victoria. He waved Bentley over without getting out of the car. The officers went back inside the house. Bentley walked around to the driver's side of Jones' car.

"Unusual to see you at a crime scene," said Bentley.

"I'm out supervising my people," said Jones. "We do that sometimes, us ell-tees. It's what we get paid for."

"Fair enough," said Bentley.

"You know, on nice days like this, sometimes I take a second lunch. I think I might do that today." He glanced at his watch. "In about twenty minutes, I'm gonna park by the old firehouse on Salinas Street. Then I'm gonna take the battery out of my cell phone. Then, I'm gonna walk over to Main Street and have lunch."

"I see," said Bentley. "Any place in particular?"

"You know that little alleyway between Main and Monterey? On the two hundred block? Well, there's a little café back there. I think the guy that runs it is named Bob something."

"Used to own the Chess club."

"Till it burned down. He closes from lunch around two-thirty, and opens for dinner and backgammon around six-thirty. But I think he might let me in anyway."

"Enjoy," said Bentley. "Anything else you'd like to tell me?"

"Bishop to king's knight two." He put the car in reverse and rolled away from Bentley, then put it into gear and drove past him towards Alvin Drive.

"Well, fianchetto," said Bentley.

Bentley tapped on the glass door of the café. The Roman blind that covered the glass moved slightly. Then the door opened about the width of a fist.

"We open for dinner at 6:30," said a heavy man in a white tee-shirt and apron.

"King's bishop to N2," said Bentley.

"Close enough," said the large man. He opened the door and stepped aside. When Bentley was inside, he closed the door and threw the bolt.

Jones sat at a corner table by the window, with his back against the wall. He was sipping coffee. Like the door, the plate glass window was obscured by a thin white Roman blind.

"Where's your cell phone?" asked Jones.

"In the glove box of my unmarked, outside the coffee shop on Main Street."

"Two hundred block?"

"Three hundred. Where the college kids hang out."

"Good call," said Jones. He paused while the proprietor put a plate in front of him. It featured a sandwich of some kind and onion rings. "You should try this. Fried chicken breast and ranch dressing on sliced sourdough."

"I was hoping for the Fugu special."

"Just sandwiches these days," said the proprietor. "Though now that you mention it…"

"I'll try what he's having," said Bentley.

"Coffee?"

"Sure."

Jones dabbed at an imaginary bit of dressing on his lip and looked at Bentley. "So, I can't tell you what the deal is. You know that, right?"

"It's your dime," said Bentley. "Talk about anything you like. I hear the Giants are looking at a new pitcher for 2024. College kid with a red-hot slider that would make this guy jealous."

"Bob's sliders are grand slams," said Jones. "But you want to know about Yorga. So here's the deal: There's a task force starting up. Seems a welder over at the city yard got arrested for stealing some of the guns he was supposed to destroy."

"I haven't heard anything about that."

"It's being kept quiet. You call and ask, his boss will say he's out sick. But he's down at county, in isolation."

"Okay, and where does Yorga come in?"

"Well, seven of the missing guns came from some of his old cases."

"Missing guns. There are guns actually missing?"

"Well, that's why there's a State task force. Because nobody knows what's missing." He ate some more of the sandwich while Bentley thought about it.

"So, how do seven unknown-if-they're-missing guns relate to Yorga? I would think … Oh. So the State task force is on it because seven guns turned up in other criminal cases, and the serial numbers traced to guns destroyed on Yorga's watch."

"Bingo. Plus, it turns out that Yorga and this welder were both members of the Gonzales Helvetic Gun Club."

"Yorga's Czech, not Swiss."

"I'm not on the membership committee," shrugged Jones. "The point is, I want you to be on the task force. I need someone who is going to keep me in the loop."

"A mole, in other words." A sandwich appeared in front of him, and he looked down at it.

"There's one small problem," said Jones.

"Me and Yorga are part – were partners."

"Bingo. So I need for you to give every indication that you really wished you were partners with anybody other than Yorga. I'm gonna put you with Kojiro. Make sure you tell him – often – that he's a big improvement on your last partner."

"You want me to talk smack about Yorga behind his back. That's the message?"

Jones finished the sandwich and wiped his hands on the napkin. "Yeah, pretty much," he said. "Also, listen for anything pertaining to a safe house or storage facility."

"Anything else I can do for you? Ivy Bells, maybe? The Venona transcripts? Enormoz? Three cigars and Special Order 191? Blueprints of the Norden bombsight? Washington's order of battle?"

"Give it a week," said Jones. "I think you'll see why I got you onto the task force. And I think you'll agree with me." He drained his coffee and then walked to the door, where the proprietor let him out.

When Jones was gone, the cook held the door and looked at Bentley. "You want that wrapped up to go?"

Kojiro – Joe Kojiro to his Asian friends, and Yoshi Kojiro to his non-Asian friends – was typing on his cell phone when Bentley found him in the Police Station break room. He frowned. "Where you been?" he asked.

"Didn't know I was working with you," said Bentley.

"Jones hasn't told you yet? No wonder this place runs so slow." He finished a text message and looked up at his prospective partner. "We're supposed to go out to Chualar."

"We don't cover Chualar," said Bentley. "That's in the Sheriff's territory."

"Yeah, they don't have anybody, and it's related to a case we're working on. So we're cool."

"Wow. A new partner, and a new case, and a trip to lovely downtown Chualar, all in five minutes or less. Be still my beating heart." He pointed to Kojiro's cell phone. "At least you know how to use those things. My last partner had thumbs the size of your elbow. Couldn't text to save his life."

"Real gorilla, huh?"

"One time he texted me 'Boring. Add Sage.' Turns out he wanted me to meet him at the corner of Boeing and Osage."

"Cool," said Kojiro, typing with his thumbs again.

"I hope it's okay if I drive."

Kojiro didn't answer, but he followed Bentley to the car. He continued stroking his cell phone and occasionally poking it with his forefinger.

"So," asked Bentley, as he buckled his seat belt. "What's the deal on this Chualar thing?"

"Search warrant," said Kojiro. His solemn face suddenly lit up at something on the screen. Then it returned to the impassive mask it had been before.

"And it's related to our case," said Bentley. "And what exactly would our case be?"

"Jones said you're on the task force now." Kojiro put away the cell phone. "You know all about the state task force, right?"

"I just barely heard about it. So what's the deal?"

"Somebody in the SPD was selling guns that were supposed to be destroyed. It's top secret."

"But you're telling me."

"You're one of us now."

"Ominous thought. So how do they know we're not in on it?"

"They've got a logarithm that tells them who's likely to be dirty. We both passed."

"I hope it's really an algorithm," said Bentley. "I was never much good at higher math."

"Logarithm, algorithm," said Kojiro, giving Bentley a look. "You knew what I meant."

"Hey, no disrespect intended. My last partner had to take off his shoes to play tic-tac-toe." He took the John Street onramp for 101 South.

"Yeah, I heard a bunch of stories about that guy. They got a warrant out on him. He was dirty, too."

"Yorga?" Bentley managed to look surprised while wishing he could backhand Kojiro and make it look like an accident.

"The algorithm – ALGORIthm – said he was 85% likely to be involved, 70% likely to be the guy behind it all. And this morning he goes missing, just about the time we bust his partner."

"His partner?" said Bentley, raising an eyebrow.

"Yeah… Well, not you, obviously. The guy that was supposed to be melting the guns. Herb something or other. Sounded German."

"Might have been Swiss. There's a lot of Swiss on the farms in the South County."

"One less, now," smirked Kojiro.

"No. Don't do that," said Bentley. "You don't arrest somebody and make it into a joke."

"The guy was stealing guns and selling them," said Kojiro, with righteous indignation. He pulled his phone out of his pocket and starting thumbing it again.

"I didn't mean anything by that," said Bentley. "I'm just saying, you know, we need to be professionals."

Kojiro lowered the phone. "Yeah. Look, I've only had my gold shield for a week, okay, and I know that makes me look green. My old man was a detective over in Visalia. I know what's what, and I'm not gonna step on my shoelaces."

"What did you do before this?"

"I was on patrol in Watsonville, then I got a gig in property here on the SPD. When this task force thing came up, I was all over it. And here we are."

"Here we are," repeated Bentley. "So, what exactly are we doing again?"

"The state people will be down at the scene," said Kojiro. "They'll fill us in. Really, we're mostly here to show that the SPD is involved in all this, too."

The house in question proved to be a farm out towards Chualar canyon. It was a remote little place, accessible by a dirt road that cast up clouds of fine tan dust as they rolled along the edge of a field of row crops. From the blue-green leaves and the short, thick stalk, Bentley guessed at brussels sprouts.

In the middle of a field, several buildings formed a farm. There was no barn, which left Bentley a little disappointed. Farms should have barns. Instead, there were several sheds, each with a corrugated metal roof that slanted a few degrees towards the fields. Some of these were fully enclosed, others open on one side, and one with no walls at all.

In the sheds, there were old trucks, several tractors, and a variety of rusty farm equipment, along with a few bizarre machines that Bentley couldn't identify. He assumed that it all had to do with agriculture. A thick layer of dirt covered the horizontal surfaces.

Across the open space between the buildings, there was a forty-foot length of barbed wire fence. It served no purpose that Bentley could imagine, but it had clearly been there for a very long time. The posts were gray from the weather, and the once-square sides featured deep furrows, carved by decades of rain and wind. The barbed wire itself was the old style: Two rusty strands of wire punctuated by tightly-wound coils, the ends protruding and pointed.

Bentley couldn't help wondering why there was a forty-foot fence in a spot where it could only be an obstacle. Was it part of a much longer fence that had been ripped out? If so, why wasn't it ripped out at the same time?

The only spot on the entire farm that didn't have a light coat of surface rust, or a layer of fine dust, was the farmhouse itself. At a crisp fifty feet from the front porch, the dirt abruptly stopped, and a precisely-cut lawn began. Where the farm was dusty and dry, the lawn was thick, lush, and so well defined that it could have been in Beverly Hills. It was as flat as the flight deck of an aircraft carrier, and only slightly less well-maintained.

Bentley looked at the grass, ball-field perfect, and then at the random furrows and ruts in front of the various sheds. There was a clear message in the contrast: That's where I work; this is my home.

Bentley stepped in the center of each of the square cement stepping stones. They were placed diagonally to the lawn, and each was as flat and level as the lawn itself. They were set slightly below the grass, so that a lawnmower could pass over them smoothly and without incident. Planning and precision. Pride of ownership.

Kojiro was already on the porch. A man in a black windbreaker was making him sign a clipboard. The windbreaker featured a yellow badge-like emblem over the left pectoral. Bentley moved up to join him and signed into the crime scene.

Yorga stared out the window. Picturesque vistas of the beaches and coastline were giving way to fields and piles of rocks. In a few minutes, the train would blaze past the town of Lompoc, most famous for its lovely federal prisons. If the map in Yorga's mind was right, the train would go through the town between the two penitentiaries. If Yorga's luck ran out, he might become much better acquainted with one prison or the other.

But Lompoc would probably be too nice for Yorga. He sighed. Low security and relaxed rules? No, he'd be more likely to wind up in San Quentin or Soledad. Country-club prison was for politicians caught breaking into Washington hotel rooms, not people accused of running guns for gangs.

Better not to wind up in any prison at all. Better to make absolutely certain he was not found. Yorga sipped Amtrak coffee and thought about his next move. Four hours to show time.

It was past the end of the watch, but Bentley was still in the station. He told Kojiro that he needed to clean up some paperwork, and used the stack of file folders on his desk as an excuse. He carefully removed the various cups of untouched coffee-like substance and disposed of them while he waited for the room to empty. Kojiro started out the door at the stroke of five.

When the coast was clear, Bentley picked up a folder and walked into Jones' office, closing the door behind him. Jones looked up. "Something I can do for you?"

"Off the record, I have some concerns about this cowboy, Kojiro." He placed the folder in front of Jones. All the papers in it were blank letter-sized sheets. Jones glanced at them, then back up at Bentley. He raised an eyebrow.

"We get to that farmhouse out by Chualar, right? Well, first thing I see is a bullet hole. It's right above an armchair, about where someone's head would be. I point it out to Kojiro. You know what he says?"

Jones slowly shook his head.

"He says that when they did the raid, he thought he saw somebody. Turned out to be a shadow. I took a look anyway, no blood or anything. So it looks like he just killed the sheetrock. Went into a stud, with no collateral damage on the other side. But, I mean, that coulda been somebody."

"Anything else?"

"Lieutenant, I'm telling you that Kojiro recklessly discharged his firearm into a wall. In a suspect's house."

"We were all young once, Bentley."

"Young. Once. Are you kidding me?"

"I don't want to hear anything else about it." He nodded towards the door. Bentley stalked out of the office, careful not to slam the door. Jones lowered his head and went back to his paperwork.

Bentley scratched his head. Something about this case stank. It made absolutely no sense that – well, Bentley was certain that if he had ever discharged his firearm that recklessly, he'd have gone on suspension for a week and taken mandatory firearms re-training. But for Kojiro, it was no big deal.

He hated to think what he was thinking. Jones was never political; he hadn't been in all the time Bentley had known him. And the idea that Jones could be dirty went against all his instincts.

The farmhouse hadn't added up either. Bentley sat down at his desk and reviewed it in his mind. Beside the armchair; that's where Kojiro claimed to have found a .22 semi-automatic rifle. Common enough on farms, and great for killing gophers, rodents, and small pests. But this one had the serial number filed off.

The lab would raise it, using their tricks with acids and ultraviolet light, but that usually meant it was stolen or used in a crime. Bad news for Herb Pfalzmann. Mandatory jail time. And if it was one that he allegedly destroyed, it would be even worse. A jury that couldn't draw that line hadn't been born.

The small kitchen; an unmarked bag of white powder in a drawer. Tested positive for cocaine. More bad news. So a middle-aged farmer with no criminal history and a clean drug test record was trading guns for drugs? Or was dealing drugs for profit, but had to get his guns from the scrap metal bin?

That made no sense at all.

The drug dog had also indicated strongly on an abandoned car behind one of the sheds. It was a 1966 Chrysler Coronet, and some collector would probably have killed for a chance to restore it. Like everything else, it was coated in dirt from long years next to muddy and dusty fields.

Except for the trunk. The trunk lid had been wiped clean along the rear edge and the places where hands would normally touch. The latch had turned out to be jammed open, conveniently allowing the lid to open at the slightest touch. And inside the trunk was a collection of illegal guns, packed with another plastic bag of white powder. None of them were dusty, like they'd been in a semi-open trunk next to a field for a while. Recent. Very recent.

It was exceptionally convenient, to Bentley's mind. Glaringly, obviously, it was a set up. But Jones seemed to see nothing at all wrong with the report. Based on Bentley's last chat with him, it would not be productive to argue with the powers that be.

Bentley took the battery out of his cell phone and left both in his desk drawer while he walked out to his car.

When the train pulled into Los Angeles Union Station, Yorga was already on the lower level, waiting for the car attendant to open the door and put down the yellow step. He walked briskly, trying not to look like he was hurrying, down the ramp into the tunnel below.

At the foot of the ramp, he looked both directions. Neither was obviously the station proper, but the right looked more promising, so he turned that direction and was soon rewarded by finding himself in a concourse full of tenant shops. The other direction probably led to waiting areas and baggage rooms.

The big clock, far up the cathedral-sized walls, told him it was ten past nine. It was dark outside, and he found that comforting.

He held his course, across the famous art deco lobby, past the various waiting areas, and out into the Los Angeles night. He was safely in a big city, hundreds of miles from anyone searching for him.

Now he just needed to blend in.

Chapter Three

"CAUGHT A BREAK in the gunrunning case," said Kojiro, as soon as Bentley walked in.

"That's what we're calling our case?"

Kojiro shrugged. Bentley frowned. Yorga would have asked if Bentley thought it should be called the Lindbergh kidnapping. He missed the repartee.

"Check this out," said Kojiro, holding out his phone. "It's an ATM machine in LA. That's Yorga's card."

"Doesn't look like Yorga," said Bentley, squinting at the face on the little screen. "But that face looks familiar."

"Yeah, facial rec pulled up a name. Guy's name is John Fitzgerald Kennedy. Out of Massachusetts. No real police record to speak of. And he has no current wants or warrants. Nothing shady."

"I doubt that Kennedy guy was using Yorga's debit card," said Bentley, putting another cup of coffee on his desk. "I find that highly unlikely."

"Yeah, apparently he was a president, and he's dead. Weird that facial rec would be that far off."

"Not really."

"Huh?"

"Novelty masks. Former presidents. Nixon, Johnson, Ford, Carter, Reagan. Haven't ever seen one for JFK, but why not?"

"Oh," said Kojiro. "Yeah, now that you mention it, the eyes look wrong. Like a mask."

"Well, there you go," said Bentley.

"Drew out about sixteen hundred dollars."

"I thought the credit union had a daily limit of eight hundred dollars."

"Yeah, it looks like that's a calendar day, not twenty-four hours. So this guy here, he made two draws, one at 11:50 and one at 12:05."

Bentley wanted to ask more questions, like how Yorga got to Los Angeles, and whether any adjacent cameras, maybe from nearby shops, had caught him going to the ATM. But asking questions might make Kojiro think, and Bentley wasn't really sure that was in anyone's best interest.

To get away from Kojiro for a moment, Bentley stepped into the evidence room. Officer Tina Calucci looked up from inside the cage.

"Nothing to declare, Tina," he said.

Tina smiled. Bentley was one of the few people on the force who didn't call her "Socks," and she appreciated it. She was very tired of the nickname.

"So what brings you around?"

"Just gotta … um, hey, did Yorga leave anything without a case number? Or maybe a CI-number?"

Socks scanned her logs. "Yeah," she said. "I got nothin' here."

"Thanks anyway," he said, as he let himself back out into the hallway. If Yorga was on something deep, which was the impression Jones had given him, Yorga woulda left a trail of breadcrumbs. He would've been collecting evidence, and leaving it somewhere.

But where?

The next morning found Yorga in a quiet little café where they didn't ask questions so long as he bought coffee from time to time. His brand new cell phone – cash, and activated with a card he bought using cash – had very nicely downloaded the webcam app, and allowed him to connect to his cameras at home.

He sipped coffee and watched.

It was 10:06 AM when the door latch suddenly moved. Yorga triggered the recording, and hoped the phone's memory card would be big enough.

A small man let himself into Yorga's apartment.

He looked around, made sure he was alone, and then closed the door gently behind him. As Yorga watched, the furtive little man slipped a pistol down behind the cushion of Yorga's armchair.

Yorga flipped to a different camera as the intruder sprinkled a fine white powder in the hallway and then stepped on it to grind it into the carpet. In the hall closet, Yorga was awarded a small rifle – likely a .22 – and a bag of fine white powder. Yorga guessed that it probably wasn't baking soda.

So, powder in the carpet to make sure that the drug dog indicated; powder in the closet with enough weight to make Yorga a trafficker. Nicely set up.

The closet was also home to Yorga's security camera system. As Yorga watched, the little man expertly opened the digital video recorder and removed the hard disk drive. Yorga shook his head. The guy probably thought that he had removed all the evidence of his visit.

With Yorga set up to join Herb Pfalzmann in the county jail, the intruder let himself out of Yorga's apartment and carefully locked the door behind himself.

Yorga stopped the recording, but kept watching. The visitor knew exactly where to find the video system, and exactly how to render it useless. Yorga found that very suspicious. Inside information.

At the time, it had seemed redundant and a bit paranoid, but in retrospect, Yorga was glad he had invested in a second camera system.

"I didn't do nothing," said Pfalzmann. "And how come you're here? What the – where's my lawyer?"

"This is off the record," said Bentley. "We don't need your lawyer as long as we're just two guys chatting."

"Except you're on that side of the glass and you got a badge," said Pfalzmann. "Irregardless, I don't gotta talk to you." He crossed his arms defiantly.

"I used to be Yorga's partner."

"Pfft. That supposed to soften me up? He sold me out. I told him something was fishy. He said to trust him. This is where it got me."

"Better than where it coulda been. So listen, on the day that you got arrested, Yorga went missing. Any idea where he went?"

"No, but I could make a suggestion where he can go. And you too, for that matter."

"Okay, you told Yorga something was fishy. What was fishy about it?"

"I told Yorga that I checked all the paperwork, and it said I signed off on more guns than I really burned. I write 10, that zero turns into a six. I write 1, it turns into a

French 7. And I showed him that one cannon I burned, that whatcha-callit Lahti thing, turned out the receiver was plastic. Weights in it, tiny little fishing weights."

"You showed it to Yorga?"

"Months ago. Gave him the blob of burnt plastic."

"What did he say?"

"Wanted to start an investigation. Get his Lt. into it. Put a big target on my forehead. I told him to go fish."

Bentley leaned back. He scratched his chin.

"Listen," said Pfalzmann. "I gotta go. Word gets out I'm talkin' to you, we're both in trouble. There's some scary guys in here, and they do people favors."

"I hear you," said Bentley. "I was never here, and we never talked." He stood up and slid off the stainless steel stool. A guard appeared at Pfalzmann's shoulder and grabbed his bicep.

Bentley walked down the narrow room, past the half-dozen windows, with their neatly mounted telephones. There were no other visits taking place.

He handed his visitor card to the Corrections Officer, who duly noted the time out and filed it in a card file. It was a risk, Bentley knew, because it established that he had spoken to Herb. A good defense attorney would look for visitor records and use it against the state's case.

It could lead to some angry people downtown, but so long as Bentley didn't use anything Herb said against him, it shouldn't be enough to spoil the case. No harm done, for now.

As soon as Bentley was out the door and walking along the asphalt path to his car, the CO picked up his phone and punched an intercom button.

"Hey, Sarge," he said, to the sheriff's sergeant that answered. "You're gonna want to hear the conversation that just happened in interview six."

Bentley had barely gotten back to the squad room before Kojiro appeared.

"Warrant," said Kojiro, waving a blue-backed paper at Bentley.

Bentley got up from his desk, careful not to dislodge the cups of cold coffee that were strategically placed on his desk.

"Who are we serving?"

"Your old partner. Franz Yorga."

Bentley kept a poker face, and walked to the car with Kojiro trailing behind him.

Yorga triggered the recording button again when he saw his door rattle in the frame. Someone was pounding on it from outside. A moment later, the door frame splintered. A detective that Yorga didn't recognize was first through the door.

Bentley was next, and Yorga wasn't sure how he felt about that. Bentley's gun was holstered, and the strap snapped shut. Yorga supposed that was some indication that Bentley was still on his side.

Kojiro rushed into the apartment, pistol in his hand. A martial arts practice dummy graced one corner of the dining room. Kojiro put a 10mm hole in its forehead. Bentley was right behind him, and snatched the hot gun out of Kojiro's hand.

"We're serving a warrant, not taking down the taliban," he snapped. He dropped the magazine into his left coat pocket and ejected the live round from the chamber. The gun, now safe, went into his right coat pocket. Kojiro scowled at him.

Bentley scanned the small apartment and verified that Yorga was not there. Then he stepped outside, where the canine officer was waiting. He was about to call Jones when his phone rang.

"Bentley," he said.

"Bentley, give Kojiro his gun back."

"Lieutenant, he shot a martial arts dummy. In the forehead. He's going to kill someone."

"We talked about this," said Jones, in a tone far too calm for Bentley's comfort. "Give him back his gun. When the search is over, come back and see me."

Bentley hung up the phone, but Jones had beaten him to it. He thumbed the rounds out of the magazine, put the empty magazine back into the gun, and manually released the slide. With the gun in his hand, he walked back into the apartment. Kojiro was standing over Yorga's kitchen table watching a technician photograph a cellophane bag of white powder.

Bentley held out the gun to him, grip first.

"Jones called you."

"Yeah, over-reacted. Sorry." Kojiro took the gun, grinning slightly. Bentley flared his nostrils and resisted the urge to punch that grin. "So what's this here?"

"Found it in his hall closet. Looks like a full kilo of fresh cocaine."

"You tested it already?"

"That's next."

"So for all you know it's baking soda."

Kojiro narrowed his eyes. "People don't keep baking soda in their hall closets."

"Most people don't keep cocaine there, either." Bentley held up his cell phone and snapped a shot of the white powder. The package looked familiar. It seemed to be taped up with the same tape that he had seen on the bag seized from Pfalzmann's farmhouse. In fact, unless Bentley was mistaken, it might be the same bag.

Kojiro smirked at him. "Get a selfie with it. You want me to take a picture for you?"

"Naw, I'm good with this," said Bentley. He walked out to the car and drove away.

Yorga watched Bentley leave. He could see the tension between Bentley and Kojiro, and he understood it. If he had been home, Kojiro would have shot him. No warning, no identification. Just a bullet to the brain.

Nice to know that they were playing for keeps. And nice to know that Bentley, whichever side he was playing for, wouldn't be down for shooting Yorga without warning.

Once Bentley was gone, the technician signaled someone outside. A man in a black windbreaker jacket carried three more rifles into the house, and the technician photographed them. First they were "discovered" under the couch, behind a chest of drawers, and standing in the bedroom closet. Then they were photographed together, on Yorga's dining table, with the gun from the armchair and the bag of powder from the closet.

That was interesting. It meant that Kojiro wasn't just a useful tool. He was in the conspiracy up to his neck. Part and parcel of the setup. He wasn't building the frame, but he was holding the jig.

Kojiro and the tech seemed to be arguing over something. Kojiro walked to Yorga's closet, and he seemed to be gesturing at the DVR that the first intruder had gutted. The technician shook his head and pointed directly at the camera Yorga was watching.

Kojiro drew his backup gun and fired a single shot. His aim was dead on, and the camera went dark. Moments later, the other camera went dark as well.

Yorga stopped the recording.

The two video files – the intruder and the raid – were fairly huge, and together they filled up a 128GB micro-SD card. He couldn't email them to himself. They were bigger than most email clients would allow.

Worse: The conspirators would assume that he had been watching them, and possibly recording. They wouldn't be content to set him up. They would have to know what he knew. And they would have to make sure he disappeared.

Yorga had maybe two paychecks in his account. He could draw about another three grand if he was careful and discreet. They would leave his bank account open to make it easier to trace him, but they'd be watching it. And the last ATM he visited would be under observation. So the trick would be to access ATMs that were not staked out yet.

He thought about the JFK mask. That was a mistake: It was hot and stuffy, for one thing. It also marked him as trying to evade recognition. So from now on, he'd only draw cash with his own face showing. And he thought that he knew how to keep that from mattering in the least.

Chapter Four

"GOT ANY DOUGHNUTS filled with a hot jalepeño or haberñero jelly?" asked Bently. "Or maybe some of that Carolina Reaper?" The guy behind the counter raised an eyebrow and shook his head.

"Got jelly filled, but it's either raspberry or grape. Or we got chantilly cream."

"Just wondered," said Bentley, as he paid for the box of doughnuts. It wouldn't matter. Even jalapeño jelly wouldn't be hot enough to burn Kojiro the way Bentley wanted. And it wasn't likely they had habañero or Carolina reaper jelly. Kojiro might even like hot jellies. And there would be no guarantee he would pick the right doughnut, anyway.

How long would he have to put up with the charade, he wondered. Obviously, if Yorga got himself caught, or worse, killed, the gig was up. All the blame would be on him, and Pfalzmann would be blued and tattooed, as the saying goes.

But suppose Yorga played it smart, and went down to Mexico? Or caught a ship out of Long Beach headed for the Western Pacific? Lots of tramp freighters took passengers without asking questions, and there were many places that a man with only a moderate amount of cash could live like a king.

Eventually, the investigation would run out of steam, and the case would go cold. And Herb would still be headed for prison, and Yorga would be a fugitive forever.

So how did he know Yorga wasn't dirty?

That was a question that he had wrestled with all night long. The answer was simple, when it finally came to him. The obvious answer was that the frame was too nice, too precise, too tight. The second was almost as obvious: Yorga wouldn't sell out his friends.

Herb Pfalzmann was in jail. Either it was because Yorga set him up, or it was in spite of the best Yorga could do. And Yorga didn't sell out his friends, so it was the second one. Which meant Yorga was clean, and so was Pfalzmann.

And as Yorga would have said, now convince eleven other people and meet me in the jury box.

Kojiro was waiting when Bentley walked into the squadroom.

"Another ATM job," he declared. "San Luis Obispo. And this time he showed his face."

Bentley managed not to laugh. Yorga drawing his own money from his ATM was now a "job." And why shouldn't he show his face, since he wasn't committing a crime?

"San Luis Obispo," said Bentley. "He's headed back this way maybe, you think?"

"I've got a BOLO with the CHP, on Highways 1 and 101. Plus we're looking for his car on ArcGIS highway cameras."

Bentley froze for a second, but recovered nicely. "What car?"

"His unmarked," said Kojiro. "It hasn't been seen since he ran. What else would he be driving?"

"Good point," said Bentley. Something happened in his mind at that point. Until then, he could honestly say that despite his friendship with Yorga, everything he had done had been by the book. Up until that moment, nothing he had done or said had helped Yorga in any way.

But as of that moment, Bentley was withholding information. And if his hunch was correct, in a few minutes he'd be withholding evidence. He put the box of doughnuts on the counter, between the three-hole punch and the paper-cutter.

"Listen," said Bentley, "I had a rough night last night. Stomach's actin' up. Tell Jones I came in but I gotta go home."

"He's not gonna like that." Kojiro glanced at the box of doughnuts. "You think you got the flu or something?"

"No, more like my ulcer flaring up. I'll go home, have some milk, and I'll be fine tomorrow."

On the top level of the parking garage – the one at the corner of Monterey and Market – Bentley committed the first overt act in his entire career that could have gotten him fired. He saw a vehicle that he knew to be of interest in an ongoing investigation, and deliberately chose not to report it.

He then committed the first crime of his life. He stole evidence in an active investigation.

Yorga's unmarked was on the upper level of the parking garage, with a light dusting of dust on the windows. There was a note under the windshield wipers – probably from the garage attendant – but the exempt license plates would keep it from getting ticketed or towed away. Chances are that the attendant hadn't even made a note of it. Aside from the one under the wipers.

Bentley backed alongside the off-white Ford Crown Victoria, leaving a couple feet between his bumper and the concrete parapet. He popped his trunk lid.

The keyless entry code for Yorga's unmarked would have been changed to the SPD default code for all police cars: 00200. 200 was the street address of the Salinas PD, on Lincoln Street. The doors unlocked. A button on the dash popped the trunk lid.

In the trunk, Yorga found the paper bag that Herb had described, and the melted lower receiver inside it. Careful not to disturb the dust on Yorga's trunk, he put Yorga's car back the way he found it.

Then Bentley drove away, with evidence of a crime in the trunk of his unmarked police car.

So what did it mean? A melted gun and a missing detective, and Pfalzmann's claim that it was all a conspiracy... It could be a lot of things. Bentley needed some time to think.

There was that chess case a few years ago, the one that started and ended at the Chess Club, on Main Street. Bentley only knew one thing about chess, and he had learned it on that case: When you're winning, simplify. When you're losing, complicate.

So, should he simplify or complicate? And before he got to that, he needed an answer to the first obvious question, was there even a conspiracy?

Well, Jones' treatment of Kojiro made it look like there was. At the very least, Kojiro had some kind of lever. Bentley wondered if he needed to take a look at Kojiro's phone. Incriminating text messages, maybe? But, no, if he started getting nosy, it would just make them cut Bentley out of the loop entirely.

He had chatted with the proprietors of the Sicilian place, and the story he got there was very simple: Someone left a note on the counter addressed to Yorga. Nobody saw who left it. When Yorga came in, they gave it to him. He had a combination pizza, ate all but one slice, and threw down a twenty when he left.

So someone tipped Yorga about something that made him disappear. Next question: Fair or foul? That is, did the note warn Yorga to run away, or did it lure him into a meeting? The ATM down in LA seemed to suggest that Yorga was alive and well, but then why the JFK mask?

So if he was lured to a meeting... Bentley ran the scenarios in his head. Yorga meets with a witness in the alley behind the bike shop on Monterey, maybe... close enough that he wouldn't want to take his car. He gets shot and stuffed into a trunk. They take his ATM card. They pull out money to make it look like he's in LA. Okay, so how would they get his PIN, and what would they do with the body?

Or they miss, and he's wounded. But he doesn't call for backup, and when he goes missing, Jones doesn't want anyone looking for him. No, that idea stank. Bentley couldn't believe that about Jones, and he wouldn't.

Okay, so what if he walked out the door on his own?

He left town. The means was pretty obvious to Bentley. He was the one who told Yorga about the Coast Starlight in the first place, when they went up to Oregon that time. Salinas, LA, and San Luis Obispo were on the same tracks. In fact, from LA, Yorga could have caught the Surfrider up to SLO, used the ATM, and caught another Surfrider back to LA. If Bentley's hunch was right, Yorga's next "ATM job" would be at Needles, a small town near Arizona.

The Southwest Chief would bring Yorga into Needles at 25 minutes past midnight, and he would have another 25 minutes to visit an ATM before catching the westbound train back to LA. Needles had the additional advantage of being on the route that a person would take by car, if he were headed East on Interstate 40. So Yorga's last bank job would suggest he was escaping the state in a car. Nice. Subtle.

Bentley assumed it would be his last ATM job. If he kept it up, someone would notice the star pattern, with LA at the center, and they'd flood LA with officers. Also, he didn't know how much Yorga had in his account, but it couldn't be enough for more than a couple more big withdrawals.

So where did that leave him?

Well, Bentley was fairly certain, based on the ATMs, that Yorga left town of his own will. So the note wasn't a setup. It was a warning. That only left one question to answer:

Was Yorga a dirty cop?

No. Whatever Pfalzmann might think – and sitting in the county jail could probably make a man very cynical – Yorga was not a dirty cop. Bentley had known him too long to suspect that Yorga could even harbor the thought of corruption. So that meant Yorga was running for his life, and Pfalzmann was in danger as well.

Bentley's musings, along with a few random turns, had placed him on San Vicente, approaching Blanco. He was, in theory, at home with an ulcer problem. No one would be looking for him for a while. He turned the wheel right and headed for the peninsula.

Yorga sat on the low stone wall that separated San Diego's Mission Beach from the broad sidewalk behind it. He stared toward the ocean and watched the sunset while he thought about his next move. Behind him, people walked, strolled, and roller-skated past.

San Diego had several advantages. It put him at the junction of two train systems: Amtrak's Surfrider and San Diego's light rail. Going one way, for a reasonable fee he could be in one of the world's largest cities within a couple hours, or anywhere along the SoCal coast. Going the other way, he could easily reach the Mexican border and be out of the country. On top of that, the SoCal weather was very nice. Might be a good place to retire, if he lived that long and kept control of his pension.

He had a good idea who he was up against. There had to be a couple of people in the SPD. Jones wasn't one of them, or Yorga hoped he wasn't. But someone was picking and choosing which guns were actually destroyed, and which guns were only destroyed on paper. There also had to be a couple of folks at the public works yard who could re-direct Herb's paperwork. There had to be some people receiving the guns and reselling them.

So where were the guns going?

If it were Yorga doing it, he'd sell them somewhere as far from California as possible, to make them harder to trace. Unless there was someone in the California DOJ who was in on it, who could make serial numbers vanish from databases, any of these guns that wound up in California would point right back to Salinas.

Mexico? That would be like sending sand to the Sahara. Yorga was fairly certain that within fifteen minutes of setting foot in Tijuana, he could obtain enough guns to arm a small revolution.

The East Coast was almost as bad. Not only were there legal dealers within easy driving distance of each gun-free state, there were enough underground guns to make competition fierce.

Overseas? Japan? Again, it would be a long way to go for a slim profit. Yorga was sure that the Yakuza might pay nicely for secondhand guns, but they would expect nearly-new guns of very specific high-end types. They would not be looking for cheap guns.

Canada?

Maybe. There was probably demand. The Canadian customs officers were pretty strict. Many Americans with concealed carry permits had learned the hard way that Canada was very serious about its gun policies. Even transiting from Washington to Alaska by land was risky for hunters who didn't jump through all the hoops.

Still, there were large shipments of freight by sea and by rail every day. No one would think twice about a couple hundred pounds of guns concealed in a few tons of computer parts.

Yorga made a mental note to add shippers to the list of conspirators.

Sandip watched intently as the man on the screen withdrew money from the ATM. He was an exceptionally large man, and Sandip realized that he hoped never to meet the man in person. He looked like a refrigerator, large and solid. The cold dispassionate eyes told Sandip that this man had seen violence and did not fear it.

And that was enough to make Sandip very glad of the hundreds of miles that separated them, and the big screen TV that insulated him from physical contact.

Xeng's assessment was less personal. Where Sandip saw a very dangerous man, Xeng saw a mark. Yorga was nothing but a victim, a mug, a punter. He existed to be set up and sacrificed, to appease the need for a scapegoat. It would be Yorga who had stolen the guns, with the help of his friend in the city yard. It would be Yorga who transported the guns and sold them overseas. Yorga, who would fall victim to his own greed, and be shot by his clients in a deal gone bad.

The clip ended, and Xeng was left staring at the last image of Yorga's retreat from the ATM.

"Where was this taken?" he asked.

"Barstow. It's near the borders of Arizona and Nevada. Not far from Las Vegas." The mildly bored pronouncement came from the third man in the room. He was fat, slightly bored, and lethargic.

The last attribute, lethargy, was what made him perfect for this job. When he moved slowly, his colleagues thought he was being casual under stress.

He sat at a long, narrow, folding table arrayed with a variety of monitor and electronic cables. He perched on a Samsonite folding chair that was barely adequate for his size, and he studied the screens with a disinterested look.

"Is it along the same route as Needles?" asked Xeng.

"Next stop."

"And did you match it to a schedule?"

"My next task," Chuck growled. "Yoshi barely sent the video an hour ago. I'm not a magician."

"Well?" asked Xeng.

"Keep your shirt on, Lou." The schedule for the Southwest Chief appeared on the screen. "Okay, arrives

Barstow 9:56 PM Eastbound. He could catch a return train westbound at 3:39 AM."

"How do we know that he was returning?" asked Sandip. "Perhaps he continues onwards eastbound to escape. After all, he would cross the state line in another two and a half hours."

"Only if he stayed on the train. Getting off at Barstow would mean waiting 24 hours to go east, but only five and a half to go back to the west."

"If getting back onto the train were his criterion for the stop, then he would be choosing Needles, where the stop would be only twenty-six minutes."

"And if the train were delayed, there goes the plan. Plus, that only gives him twenty-six minutes to get off the train, find an ATM, use it, and get back on the westbound train." Chuck squinted at Sandip. He might be smart, but there were times when the skinny Indian didn't make a lot of sense.

"You're both idiots," snapped Xeng. "If he were going east he'd wait until the train takes on fuel and water at Albuquerque. He'd have thirty minutes, and he could catch the same train."

Sandip wasn't ready to drop it. "How are we knowing that he was not traveling by car?" He made a small hand motion, and Chuck grudgingly put a map on the screen. "Here is Barstow, Needles, Kingman. If he is following the I-40 eastbound, he is going directly through each of these cities, same as riding the train."

"Because he doesn't have a car," said Chuck. "Fled by train, hasn't rented a car."

"Perhaps he uses cash to be buying a used car or to be renting one."

"Fool's move if you're trying to get lost," said Xeng. "Cars are easily traceable. Trains, in America, are nearly invisible." Xeng touched the map on the display, just over the city of Los Angeles. "All the places we know he's been to; they all connect here, at Los Angeles. First Salinas, then San Luis Obispo, Los Angeles, now Barstow. Train rides out and back."

"So he's hiding in Los Angeles," said Chuck, as if that settled the matter.

"No." The reply was weary, as if Xeng could not imagine how Chuck managed to find his way home at night. "He will not be in Los Angeles, because that is where all the trains converge. He is no fool. He will be a short train ride away, in another large city where it is very easy to hide."

Xeng's finger moved down the map and tapped twice on the city of San Diego. "Close enough to LA and the trains there. Close enough to the border of Mexico, should he need refuge. Close to three major interstate highways. And a lovely place to sit and wait."

Chuck frowned. Xeng was right.

"How long will it take us to drive down?"

"If we leave now…" Sandip consulted his watch. From Santa Clara, down US 101, no commuters at this time of night, more than half the length of the state – Call it five hundred miles?

"Perhaps ten hours, and perhaps less, if we are going over the Pacheco Pass to the Golden State Freeway. Getting there at perhaps five, six?"

"It's a little bit less direct, but probably faster," conceded Chuck. "Especially with the traffic."

"You're staying here," said Xeng. "Sandip and I will handle this matter. See if Yoshi gets anything else for us, and text us updates."

Chuck shrugged. "You're the boss, Lou."

Xeng looked over his shoulder as he and Sandip walked out of the warehouse. Chuck did not look like a professional, he thought to himself.

Chuck was overweight, slovenly, and full of himself. His computer skills and his lack of a working conscience were not enough to justify his laziness and insolence.

When this present crisis was all over, perhaps the team would need to trim the fat. Xeng smiled at his own joke and climbed into the car beside Sandip.

Chapter Five

YORGA BEGAN HIS morning routine the usual way. First, he listened intently for anything or anyone who shouldn't be there. Then he got out of bed and made the rounds of the apartment, checking the doors and peering sideways through the edges of the blinds. As usual, the apartment was undisturbed, but he kept his ears open and his pistol near as he showered, shaved, and dressed.

"You can stay if you want," Earl had said. "I'm gonna be down fishing off Baja. Wish you'd given me some heads-up about coming down to visit. We coulda had dinner, talked about the old times."

"Didn't know I was coming till I got here. One of those things where you just have to get away for a while."

"Don't I know it. I retired just about when it was gonna make me nuts. Best thing I ever did. Hey, you're still here when I get back, we gotta catch up. Who's doing what, where's ol' so-and-so."

"If I'm still here. I might go see an old girlfriend out in Kingman, if I start feeling lonely."

"Not that Mauri woman again, right? Come on. She was trouble, Franz. Nothin' but trouble."

"Not Mauri," he had said, and then he had watched Earl Licowicz, retired SPD lieutenant, climb into an old Chevy station wagon and putter off. And that left Yorga with a nice anonymous place to stay, where no one in the world would think of looking for him.

Which made him no less paranoid.

Xeng snapped awake near noon. In the other bed, Sandip lay with his mouth wide open. Xeng was mildly surprised that no one had called to complain about the noise. Sandip's snoring could shake the paint off the walls.

The noise – the noise that was not Sandip – repeated itself. Three sharp taps – The edge of a plastic card against the door. Someone outside was yelling something, but the high pitch of the voice made it impossible to discern.

Xeng drew on his pants as the tapping repeated. With the chain at its full length, he saw the housekeeper outside.

"Twelve o'clock," she insisted. "Checkout time."

She was nearly right. They had ten minutes or so before the management tried to charge them double.

"We will be out in a minute," he said. "My friend is still asleep. Ten minutes."

"Ten minutes," she agreed.

He closed the door and shook Sandip's arm.

Yorga remembered something someone had once said about war, something about it being lengthy boredom punctuated with brief moments of sheer terror. Bentley probably could have quoted it and then told him who said it. Regardless, it fit this situation.

If he hadn't been scanning the crowd, looking for someone who didn't fit in, Yorga might have enjoyed himself. He had a nice cup of coffee beside him as he sat on a nice veranda overlooking Mission Beach.

They'd never think to look for him here – a borrowed apartment in a borrowed city – but that didn't stop him from keeping a running tally of the number of people who came by more than once.

Maybe he'd use Earl's other car and go out for a while. It was an ancient little Honda, made for two people, but only if they were very friendly. The rear window had a huge oversized gasket around the glass. He had the vague impression that it was only offered that way for one year.

Maybe him and the Honda would go down to Petco Park and watch the Padres. Maybe he'd get something to eat in a fast-food place at Horton Plaza. If he was feeling nostalgic, he might even drive down to Thirty-second Street and PacFleet station to see if any of the scenery had changed over the years.

Or he might spend another day watching TV and going out of his mind while he waited for someone to try and kill him. He scanned the room again, hoping some kind of reading material would appear, but it didn't. Not even a TV Guide.

Bentley was not having nearly so casual a day. The barista hadn't put the lid on his coffee correctly, and as a result it had dribbled all over his shirt and tie. He had a fresh tie – he kept one in the car – but the shirt was a lost cause. He'd have to keep his jacket buttoned.

And then he had to watch Kojiro practically jumping up and down with excitement over the latest Yorga sighting. You'd have thought Yorga was Elvis or something. That made him idly wonder if he had ever seen Yorga wear suede shoes, blue or otherwise.

"Cold-blooded," said Kojiro, fiercely eyeing the computer screen. "Look how calm he is. He walks right up to the ATM as if he owns it."

"Instead of, you know, just owning some of the money in it."

Kojiro gave Bentley a look. He was getting a bit tired of the detective's smart remarks.

"Lab says it was cocaine," he said. "In that bag in Yorga's apartment. Same as the Swiss guy."

"Same blend, same ratios of impurities?" asked Bentley. He wouldn't have asked Yorga, but he figured Kojiro might need a bit of prompting.

"Exactly the same," said Kojiro, with wide eyes and a wry grin. "Exactly the same."

It was dark when Yorga came down the ramp out of the parking garage at Horton Plaza. The Padres had lost an afternoon game to the Giants – no surprise there – and then Yorga had immersed himself in commerce. An early dinner in Horton Plaza, a little bit of walking around in the mall, and finally a movie to round out the night.

More importantly, he had visited a bookstore – an honest-to-goodness brick-and-mortar bookstore – and had obtained several magazines and a couple of books. As nice as it was that Earl had lent him the apartment, he really wished that Earl had been a more avid reader.

Yorga wasn't that much of a reader himself, but watching TV all day and all night was starting to wear on him. If he wound up staying here long term, he'd have to find some amusements. Maybe go to the zoo, see the wild animal park, things like that.

Without planning it or even realizing it, Yorga found himself on Harbor Boulevard, looking at the familiar sites. It had been many long years, but there was the Marriot Marquis hotel, dominating the skyline – Yorga still remembered it as the Hotel Intercontinental, its name when he lived in San Diego.

There wasn't much traffic. He could only see one car behind him, some distance back. He allowed himself to cruise along at a leisurely pace.

Across the long, narrow bay that ran parallel to Harbor Drive, Coronado Island hosted a couple of carriers – Yorga couldn't identify them; it had been too long. Not the Kitty Hawk, and not the Midway. Those ships had long since gone to pasture.

A tall bridge carried Highway 75 over the channel, connecting I-5 to the island. The bridge blazed with white LED streetlights. Yorga remembered them being orange, from the high-pressure sodium lamps of the eighties. Time and technology, always moving forward.

As he went under the bridge to North Island, Yorga became aware of a car close on his bumper, with high beams. He moved into the right lane to let the car pass.

Harbor drive jogged slightly east. Barrio Logan was coming up, a mostly industrial area, with shipyards on the ocean side and warehouses inland. The other car drew alongside him, and Yorga saw the window roll down just as he reached Sampson Street.

Instinct took over. Yorga stomped the brakes and yanked the wheel right, just making the corner at Sampson. Two flashes of light, two snapping sounds, two pings off of the corrugated warehouse on the corner. A second later on the brakes and he'd have been dead.

He killed his lights in the shadows that covered the road and he snapped the wheel left, making a forty-five into a narrow set of ruts alongside a dark railroad spur. He could barely see them in the near-dark, but he kept his foot off the brake to avoid giving himself away.

The disused spur crossed Sampson Street on a diagonal, and the ruts led to an informal parking lot, a patch of dirt convenient to the FESSCO drydocks. The ruts were the unofficial side entrance to the unofficial parking lot.

In the dim light, he nestled his car between a pair of SUVs and sat quietly, watching the narrow track he had followed. He carefully checked that his foot was off the brake pedal.

They would double back. And they did. He saw their lights as they went down Sampson past the railroad spur. The track and the ruts were visible in the daylight, but impossible to see in the dark; not unless you knew them well. Sampson Street was very dark at night, lit mostly from streetlights on Harbor Drive.

Through the other cars, he caught a glimpse of his attackers as they turned around where Sampson ended on Belt Drive, at a gray sheet metal warehouse. Then back up Sampson, slowly, past the spur again. He could almost sense the argument they must be having: hissed accusations and whispered orders at each other.

They came back again, up Sampson to Harbor, then back down Sampson to Belt Drive, along the shipyards. Yorga could not have vanished.

He couldn't have spun around and doubled back on Harbor Drive; they would have seen him. But he wasn't jetting down Belt Drive, or they'd see his taillights.

Those had to be the thoughts bouncing around inside their heads. They'd be wondering how he pulled off his disappearing trick. And there was a chance that they might stumble onto the ruts alongside the spur.

Yorga tried to figure out what he would do next if he were in their places. It seemed like an impossible dilemma for them. They couldn't cover all the bases at once.

If they stuck around by Harbor and Sampson, guarding the main road, there was the danger that Yorga knew some secret way around it and had already escaped. Maybe one of the shipbuilders' warehouses opened up further down, past the bridge, where Yorga could make his way up past Petco Park and lose them in small side streets of Barrio Logan.

On the other hand, if they tried to thread their way through the warehouses, stopping to search the parking areas, they ran the risk of letting him slip back up Sampson and out into Barrio Logan from that direction. Without backup, they couldn't plug all the holes, and they couldn't search for him.

And in either case, they ran the risk of encountering a security patrol. With a car that smelled of gunpowder, and a freshly discharged pistol under the seat, roaming around in shipyards used by defense contractors, they couldn't run the risk. The entire plan hinged on killing Yorga without leaving evidence that he had been set up, so any kind of confrontation that left evidence or witnesses was simply impossible.

Yorga watched them leave, quickly this time. On foot, he slipped over to the track and then edged along in the shadows till he could see the entire block. They were completely gone.

Just to be safe, Yorga waited another ten minutes before he slipped the bright yellow, and very distinctive, Honda out of its hiding place and driving down near the warehouses. Belt Drive became Dewey, and after snaking through among the warehouse parking areas, it left him on Chavez Parkway, behind Petco Park.

He drove cautiously back to Mission Beach, staying in the shadows as much as possible, following the back streets until Earl's car was safely hidden in the parking garage behind Earl's apartment.

Yorga slept fitfully all that night, listening for his assassins. Several times, he woke up, took the pistol from his bedside table, and prowled through the apartment, looking for any sign of life. There was nothing in the dark except darkness.

He took a blanket and a pillow from the bed, creating a small nest for himself in the aisle between the bed and the wall. It might give him a couple more seconds to wake up and shoot. Except to wake up he'd have to sleep, and that wasn't happening.

When he finally fell into a deep slumber, he dreamed of not making the turn onto Sampson quite fast enough. He dreamed of chasing his assassins down on foot. He dreamed of being hunted and cornered. And he finally woke up to daylight streaming through the windows.

The morning routine was a bit slower this time, and he spent a little more time peering around the curtains and sweeping the beach with his eyes before he emerged from the apartment. He took a different route to the coffee shop, and managed to get back to the apartment with the San Diego Tribune in record time.

There was no mention of shots fired near the FESSCO shipyards, and no mention of a fugitive yellow Honda. No mention of a wanted man hiding in the Mission Beach area. Well, of course not; the paper would have already gone to bed when the assassins took their potshots at him.

But an item in the personals caught his eye.

FYi: Collide-o-scope.

The FY in capitals was what did it. FYI might mean
"For Your Information," but FY were his initials. The
message itself proved that the message was for him.

He scoured the apartment looking for a computer,
and his search was in vain. Earl was old-school, from the
days when police work meant paper and notebooks. In
fact, Yorga suspected that having to use computers was
part of the impetus for his retirement.

It would be the library, then. And he would only use
public transportation to get there. Earl's yellow Honda
was a magnet for bullets, and Yorga felt allergic to lead.

Kojiro had a grin that made Bentley grit his teeth, but
he managed to keep a smile on his face as he walked into
the squadroom.

"Can you believe it?" asked Kojiro. "The man's got a
warrant, he's hiding from police, and he goes to a ball
game. Look, there, in the stands."

On the screen, the camera panned the crowd,
focussing on a pair of hopeful children wearing bright
orange Giants hats and holding outfielder mitts. Two
rows behind them, Yorga was clearly visible, eating a hot
dog. Bentley watched to see if Yorga would speak to the
camera, but that was silly. How would he know that the
camera would be on him? And what would he say?

"Too late now," said Bentley, shrugging it off.

"Witnesses saw a man fitting his description get into
a yellow compact car. Sub-compact. Bright yellow."

"Yorga, in a sub-compact car? You've actually met
him, right?"

"No, and I'm just telling you what the reports say."

"Okay, no need to get testy over it. Any luck tracing the car?" he asked, hoping the answer was "no."

"Apparently they lost it. But SDPD are trying to get witnesses to ID the make and model. It was a very unique car, kind of rare. Distinctive rear window."

Bentley suppressed the urge to tell Kojiro that a car could be unique or not unique, but not very unique or sort of unique. Talking to Kojiro was sometimes like listening to fingernails on a chalkboard.

Jones had said to be nice. He would be nice. He kept telling himself that he would be nice while he walked to the break room and got another cup of horrible coffee.

The collide-o-scope was the nickname that Bentley and Yorga had given to a local traffic camera in the neighboring town of Monterey, at the corner of Foam and Reeside Streets. Tourists coming around the corner from the tunnel, staring at the suddenly-visible harbor, tended to run the red light by the Coast Guard base.

The traffic camera was mounted on a pole at the corner of the Coast Guard base, to draw attention to the problem. And possibly to save a few unwary Coasties from untimely ends at the hands of reckless tourists.

It definitely provided entertainment for internet users. There was a website dedicated to video clips of crashes and close calls at that intersection. If the camera was effective in any other way, Yorga couldn't tell.

Yorga connected to the Local-Gov-Cams.Com website and typed in Monterey, California. From the list that appeared, Yorga selected the cam at the corners of Foam and Reeside.

The camera had a two-week look-back period. He wasn't sure what he was looking for, so he had to skim through several days' of old footage, mostly cars zipping through the red light, to find what he was looking for. He idly wondered if a reality TV show could be made that way. Punch up the good scenes, where pedestrians were diving for cover, and fast-forward all the rest. It held Yorga's attention, but Yorga knew there was a message in it for him, so he might not be the typical viewer.

When he saw it, he almost sped past it. Two days prior, there was Bentley standing on the corner, with the bright white wall of a motel behind him.

Rewinding slightly and slowing to normal speed, Yorga watched as Bentley held up eight fingers. Then three. Then one finger. 831, the area code for the Salinas-Monterey metro area. This would be a phone number. Yorga jotted down the digits on a slip of paper.

Yorga fished in his jacket pocket and came out with one of the burner cells he had bought in Los Angeles. Activation only took a few minutes, and then he texted the number Bentley had given him.

Alive and well, thanks for asking. Bentley hadn't asked anything, but he would understand.

BOLO yellow Honda compact. Early model, distinctive rear window. How's Earl?

Okay, that put a new spin on it. Be-On-Look-Out for the car Yorga was driving. Which Bentley knew, but obviously hadn't told anyone, belonged to Earl Licowicz. Still, it was only a matter of time before SDPD, or last night's team of would-be assassins, busted down the apartment door looking for Yorga. Or set up Earl to come home to a drug bust.

He hadn't counted on scrambling out of town so soon, but there was no avoiding it. If he wanted to live long enough to solve the case and get his life back, he would need to make tracks. Quickly.

On the brighter side, that answered the question of where Bentley's loyalties lay. Bentley knew where he was, and hadn't given him up.

Earl is fishing off Baja. How's the weather?

There was a pause before the reply.

Inclement.

Things were a bit hot in Salinas, then. Well, he might still be able to work something out.

Moving Day. Need to go and pack.

Travel light. And move fast.

Yorga turned off the cell and removed the battery.

Chapter Six

SANDIP TRIED TO shift his weight so that the pistol didn't dig into his side. The carved wooden seats at the train station were hard and rigid, and were obviously not made for a man with a pistol tucked under his belt.

"Excuse me, Sir," asked the Amtrak policeman. Sandip looked up at him. "Do you have a ticket? The seats here, in this part of the terminal, are reserved for passengers with tickets."

"I am waiting to be meeting later with my wife," lied Sandip. "She will be bringing all of the tickets when she comes here."

The Amtrak policeman frowned. "She needs to be here within the next fifteen minutes, or else I'll have to ask you to just move along. These seats are for ticketed passengers only."

Sandip shifted again in the uncomfortable seat. It was a perfect vantage point for watching the ticket window, but if he had to move, he could go sit at the small coffee stand and watch the doors to the trains instead.

The Amtrak policeman gave no sign of seeing the pistol, and instead walked casually away from the seating area. When he was out of Sandip's range of vision, he keyed the mike that was clipped to his epaulet.

"I have a suspicious male, dark skin, possibly Asian Indian, carrying a concealed weapon. Request backup, and closure of the main seating area. We may have to have a confrontation."

Xeng parked the car about three blocks from the apartment. It would have been better to make the entry at night, but he could not afford to wait. And it would have been better to have Sandip with him, but Yorga might be planning another ATM raid, or the incident on Harbor Boulevard might have spooked him. He might be running away again. The station had to be covered.

His hoodie was too warm for the late morning sun, but he had modified it by tearing off the sleeves, so that it wasn't an immediate tell. The rubber flip-flops and the baggy jeans were camouflage.

Shorts would have been better, but he couldn't bring himself to expose his pale legs. And a tee-shirt would have been ideal, except that it wouldn't hide the gun. The sleeveless hoodie would have to serve for now.

For a man accustomed to suits, slacks, and at his most casual, perhaps polo shirts, Xeng had made a major concession. He tugged down the bill of his ball cap, re-seated the cheap sunglasses on his nose, and wondered for the ten-thousandth time why no one had invented glasses with an appropriate fit for Asian faces.

He walked casually by the building on his first pass; just another tourist taking in the sights. Yorga was not on the small balcony that Earl Licowicz' apartment offered. There were no obvious signs of occupancy. No lights on, no reflections from a TV, and no obvious movement in the windows. But it was daytime, and harder to tell.

Xeng kept walking until he reached a small surf shop. He looked at skateboards in the window while he determined that he was not being followed.

Casual slow turns on the balls of his feet allowed him to confirm that no one was paying any attention to him. He satisfied himself that no one was watching. Then he began strolling back towards the apartment.

The apartment was above a tee-shirt shop, and Xeng paused by a rack of board shorts while taking a second and more thorough look at the apartment. Still no signs of life through the windows.

Time to make sure that there wouldn't ever be any.

Sandip stood up, and the discomfort went away. Standing, there was nothing pressing on the barrel of the pistol, so the butt did not dig into his lateral obliques.

He hadn't bothered with a holster. The gun rested securely under his belt, in the hollow where the side of his hip melded into his left buttock. He would be able to draw quickly if need be, reaching across himself, but the gun would stay secure and hidden.

He smoothed his windbreaker, making sure that the hem was below the bulge of the gun. Then he casually sauntered out the door towards C Street.

The sidewalk was curiously vacant around the doorway, and it did not occur to Sandip to wonder why. A man in a light gray suit got out of a parked car and jogged towards him. A businessman, late for his train, maybe. Too late, Sandip realized that the man looked like a cop, and was running straight at him.

The man in the suit pulled a gun and held it on him. Hands seized Sandip's arms from behind, forcing him down to the ground. His pistol was tugged out of its hiding place.

"You have the right to remain silent," said the man in the suit, as his comrades clicked the handcuffs into place.

Xeng used a pick-gun on the dead bolt, then used it again on the door handle. He was confident that no one inside the apartment would hear the soft but distinctive clicking, but he crouched as he gently pushed the door open, just in case.

No one was visible in the front room or the small kitchenette, so he stepped softly inside, pushing the door almost closed behind him. As a matter of habit, he stepped out of the flip-flop shoes, leaving them next to the doorway.

No one in the front rooms, no one in the bathroom, no one in the first bedroom. The second bedroom looked like someone had been sleeping there recently. The bed was carelessly half-made, the corner of the sheet and blanket tossed carelessly towards the corner of the mattress. The bed in the other bedroom had hospital corners, carefully folded and tucked, like you'd expect to see in a hotel.

In the closet of the room with the poorly-made bed, there were depressions on the carpet from the feet of a small travel bag, now missing. There was nothing personal in the closet or the nightstand. Yorga had been spooked. He was in the wind.

Xeng said a bad word, and hoped that Sandip had picked up Yorga's trail at the train station.

Sandip's phone rang. He couldn't answer it. It would be Xeng, of course, but the phone was in the plastic bag on the front seat, with his wallet and his keys. Sandip was sitting in the back seat, with his hands cuffed behind his back. His gun, now inside a plastic evidence bag, was in the suit jacket pocket of the cop who had arrested him.

Sandip leaned forward to see the phone display, but the phone was facing the wrong way, and the big red stripe across the bag obscured it. The plexiglas barrier over the seat kept him from leaning farther forward.

It didn't matter. All that the display would tell him was that Xeng was calling. He already knew that, so he leaned back and tried to get comfortable.

What he really wanted to know was whether Xeng had found Sergeant Yorga, and if so, what he had done with him. Though, at that exact moment, it was the least of Sandip's concerns.

He looked out the windows again, and was surprised to discover that he was alone. Not just alone in the car, but alone among the cars. The policemen had assumed that he was secure in the back of the car and had joined the excitement within the station.

Since there were no handles on the inside doors, and since there was a metal-mesh barrier and a plexiglas window to keep him from going over the seat, it was a fairly safe assumption.

They would need all of the available police to search the station, in case there were more men with guns. It made sense. He leaned back again, but not far enough to make the handcuffs dig into his back.

Xeng saw the police cars outside the station as he rolled by on Kettner Boulevard. Was it possible that Sandip had managed to shoot Yorga at the station? Were the police inside, standing over Yorga's body? Or were the police chasing Sandip down the platforms and out towards the airport?

He glanced at one of the police cars and was startled to see Sandip sitting calmly in the back seat. Xeng said another bad word and turned onto B Street.

He found space to park his car at the corner by India Street. The meter had ten minutes on it. Xeng checked his pockets. He had no change. But ten minutes should be plenty of time.

His overcoat was in his trunk. He tossed it over his arm and trotted diagonally through the parking structure, emerging at C Street and Kettner, next to the car in which Sandip was imprisoned.

Moments later, he had Sandip, the latter wearing the overcoat to conceal his handcuffs, and they trotted back across the parking garage to Xeng's car. They made an odd duo: one wearing an overcoat like a cape, and the other with a sleeveless sweatshirt. No one gave them a second glance.

Xeng held the door open and waited patiently as Sandip gingerly seated himself in the passenger seat. He was tempted to put his hand on Sandip's head, the way that the police do when seating a suspect. But he was concerned that it might make people realize that Sandip was handcuffed, so he didn't do it.

"Did you get him?" Xeng asked.

"No, I stepped out for some air and the police came from nowhere. They tackled me."

"He wasn't at the apartment. He must be coming here." Xeng glanced at the meter. Four minutes remaining. "Stay here," he said, closing the door and trotting back towards C Street.

"Like I am having any choice," said Sandip, under his breath. A parking enforcement cart rolled by, noting the green light on top of the meter, but not the fugitive in the passenger seat. On the next block, the cart swerved into a space between cars and the enforcement officer dismounted. Sandip watched as she scanned a license plate and then began punching buttons.

The little tablet spat out a citation, which she mounted under the wipers before climbing back into her cart and continuing East. Sandip watched her go, and breathed a sigh of relief.

Xeng strolled casually into the station, as if he planned to buy a ticket. Police were everywhere, standing in pairs by the doors, walking through the seating areas, and leading dogs along the queues of passengers waiting for trains.

He made up his mind quickly: If Yorga had come here, he was now either on a train or had fled from the police. Or he had seen Sandip, called the police, and then run away. In no possible case would he be here, waiting in a queue. It was a fool's errand to look for him here.

Xeng quietly went out the same doors he had come in. Once he was in the parking garage, and out of sight, he started trotting back towards the car. Maybe they could get ahead of the trains, if they could find what train he had gotten onto.

Yorga stood up to stretch his legs and looked around the Los Angeles bus station. The seats, molded plastic, with a yellow-on-orange pattern that made him think of orange marmalade, were making the base of his spine threaten to revolt.

He thought about walking around the station, but he wasn't sure how many cameras they had or where they were placed. Cameras were likely to be his downfall.

His plan depended in part on avoiding the two gentlemen who had tried to shoot him by the shipyards. If they knew the car, they must know the apartment where he had been staying. If they could get SDPD to put out a BOLO, they could easily run the DMV records.

There couldn't be more than one car like that in the greater San Diego area; by now they would know it was Earl's, and where Earl lived. And if they had gotten that far, they might easily have figured out that he was riding the trains, as well.

His bus for King City would be called soon. He'd have to spend a night there, in order to catch the local transit bus in the morning. It wouldn't be a bad place to stop. He seemed to recall that there was an inexpensive motel on the Broadway loop.

Across the innumerable rows and sections of the orange-marmalade molded seats, Yorga saw a small Hispanic man in a grey shirt. There was a name sewn over the pocket, but Yorga couldn't read it across the acres of seating. He watched, partly from caution, but mostly from a lack of anything more entertaining, as the man plugged a floor buffer into a wall outlet.

For a few minutes, the buffer danced back and forth on the floor, as the man expertly guided it with tiny changes to its balance. Then it stopped. The man clicked the switch several times, made a face, and walked to the outlet. After a minute, he moved the plug to another outlet on another wall. The buffer worked again, so he resumed his task.

Yorga sighed. The best he could do for entertainment was to watch a custodian buffing floor tiles?

He sat down again, and dug into his small travel bag, the same one that made the marks Xeng had seen on Earl's carpet. He fished out an Ed McBain book and started reading.

Bentley sat at his desk holding an open manila folder as if he were reading the contents. In fact, he was looking over it at his partner, whose thumbs were furiously typing. He wondered if Kojiro was playing a video game.

Kojiro said a bad word under his breath, and Bentley glanced back down at the folder. Either it was bad news, or Kojiro had lost at his video game.

Choices. It always came down to choices, and knowing the right one from the wrong one was just about impossible. He could stay on the task and collect evidence to put Kojiro away for murder and corruption, but he ran the risk of Yorga being murdered.

He could tell Jones to shove this double-agent stuff, and hand over his badge, but then Yorga was out in the cold. He could find a way to slip down to San Diego, but he'd have to find Yorga and then he'd have to guard him. Not to mention that that would give the bad guys a second target.

It seemed like the best choice was to stay where he was. He had a better chance of helping Yorga as a police detective than as a renegade civilian. So against his instincts, and against his better judgment, and despite the way it made his blood boil, he decided to stay put. For now. Just for now.

"They missed him," said Kojiro.

Bentley looked at him and raised an eyebrow.

"Yorga," explained Kojiro. "He was sighted at San Diego Union Station, but the police missed him. And he didn't get onto a train. We checked." Kojiro shook his head at the SDPD, as if wondering how they had missed so obvious and so large a target.

"I hate to be crass, and to suggest that we do some actual police work," said Jones, walking up behind them, "But has anyone here bothered to look for Yorga's unmarked car?"

Bentley looked at him with as blank a look as he could muster, then turned to face Kojiro. Kojiro stared back, but his face only expressed mild annoyance. Bentley wasn't sure if it was addressed to Jones, for suggesting actual work; at Bentley, for not having thought of it already; or at himself for not tracking the GPS. For that matter, he might have been annoyed at Yorga for inconveniencing him by not parking his car in the lot by Church Street, behind the station.

King City's Broadway has a modest but very eclectic set of businesses. Those closest to the Broadway loop bear curious resemblance to convenience stores. Past the high school, which vaguely resembles a 1930s WPA project, the architecture veers towards Soviet Brutal styles, missing the mark only through a combination of flamingo paint and the occasional parking lot planter with weeds and a scrawny tree in it.

At the end nearest the clock – once called the Meyer Tomato clock, but now simply "the clock" – there are sections of buildings with a cement boardwalk, and sections that combine aspects of boardwalk, flamingo, brutal, and convenience store.

There are liquor stores, cafés, a doughnut shop, a tire shop, two or three 99-cent shops, an assortment of Mexican cafes, an accounting office, and a hardware store, not to mention several county offices and a few boutique clothing stores.

A surprising number of the various eating and drinking establishments are named for dos, tres, or quatro siblings. As in any downtown area these days, there are even a few closed storefronts with signs wistfully declaring them available for lease.

In the third 99-cent store that he visited, Yorga found what he was hoping for, and managed to pick up a variety of accessories for it. The shopping expedition was quick enough that he wouldn't miss his local transit bus. The things he bought didn't all match. But they would serve the purpose.

Xeng sat in the security office of the Los Angeles bus depot, staring at the security screen. It was frozen on an image of Yorga going out the back door of the station in a queue of passengers. Clearly, he had boarded a bus just after that, but none of the cameras showed which bus.

The time stamp on the tape was completely wrong, and there had been at least three power interruptions since Yorga had been there. Apparently, the security system was on the same electrical circuit as one of the plugs in the lobby. This wouldn't have mattered, except for the janitor with the defective buffer.

Francisco "Pancho" Morales might have been able to take a paper and pencil, and add up how long it had taken him to reset the breaker each time it had blown. One time, he had waited until after lunch, and another time there was a plumbing problem he had to fix first. So maybe it was half an hour or so, and maybe it was three hours or more.

Plus he still had the floor to buff, right? *Argullo profesionale,* pride in his work, but this guy, *El Chino,* he wouldn't understand that. He was all *andele, andele.* Pancho didn't really care how long the power had been off.

But this pushy Chinese guy was making him angry. Giving him what he wanted didn't seem right. This guy should have more respect. So instead of giving him good information, he just frowned and shrugged, pretending not to understand.

"Yeah, I dunno," he said. He tried to give Xeng a blank look, like maybe he really didn't understand the question.

"Come on," said Xeng. "You tell me how much time." For his part, Xeng was every bit as annoyed as Pancho. Pancho – he knew the name because it was sewn on the shirt, just above the man's pocket – was simply not paying attention. Xeng was used to having people do what he said and to answer his questions quickly. A simple custodian should be eager to help him, and to win his favor and approval.

"I think maybe," Pancho said, as he looked down at his watch. "Right now it's like ten o'clock. Right?"

"No," said Xeng, "When the breaker trips, how much before you reset?"

"No, look," said Pancho, turning his wrist to show Xeng his watch. "Ten o'clock. Like four minutes to." Pancho managed not to smile at the other man's annoyance.

Xeng shook his head in frustration. This guy couldn't tell him how long the power was off. Without knowing the offset between the present time and the time shown on the screen, there was no way to guess what bus Yorga was getting onto.

Well… there was daylight reflecting off the faces. It was whiter than the tungsten indoor light. So that ruled out the night busses. Nothing too early morning, nothing late night… Which still left most of the busses. Nearly all of them.

People getting onto the busses… No, he'd need some kind of facial recognition software, and then he'd need to get the clerks to match them with manifests. And that was not going to happen.

Okay, he had it, but it was a needle in a haystack. He could look at the pattern of busses. Start counting with the first queue that had daylight reflecting off of faces. Then he'd count how many queues till he had Yorga's face on camera. One queue per bus, and all he would need then was a timetable.

But it would take him all day to scan the cameras. The solution came quickly: He'd have Sandip do it. Sandip deserved to get stuck with it, after the screw-up at the train station.

Chapter Seven

YORGA KEPT HIS head down as he got off the bus. He hadn't shaved in a few days, so the scruffy beard and the untrimmed mustache would help fool any facial recognition. Of course, they probably had photos of him from the ATMs, so it wouldn't help much. Still, any advantage is an advantage.

He kept the hoodie pulled up over his head and carried the plastic shopping bag in his left hand. His right was in the pocket of the hoodie, resting gently on his back-up pistol.

He shuffled his steps a bit, as if uncertain of his footing, and then wandered aimlessly down Central Avenue. He wanted to look drunk, and possibly homeless.

Once he was past Roosevelt school, and reasonably sure that he wasn't on any cameras, he picked up his pace to a purposeful stroll. At Lorimer he turned left, and then a couple of seemingly random turns brought him to a small set of apartments.

It had originally been a symmetrical set of two top-floor and two bottom-floor, with a common front door and inside stairs front and back. Someone had built out the backs of the bottom-floor apartments, adding a room to each. Later, the garages behind the building had been converted to a set of four studios.

Yorga was interested in the top floor apartment on the right. As he had expected, the key was still stuck to the bottom of the fire extinguisher in the hall. The alarm code was still 1986.

From the bag, he produced a small battery-powered vacuum. On the first pass, he cleaned a small area in front of the closet. Then, with gloved hands, he removed a kilogram of cocaine from its hiding place between two folded blankets inside the closet. He replaced the package with a couple of mothballs, to react with and degrade any traces of coke left on the blankets.

In the living room, a damaged and very rusty starter pistol came out from under a seat cushion, and a 12-gauge single-shot shotgun with a bent barrel came out from behind the bookcase. The shotgun wouldn't go into the bag, but the pistol fit nicely. He wrapped the shotgun with a towel and then placed it inside a garbage bag.

He was about to leave when an afterthought stopped him. He drew a cup of water from the tap in the kitchen, poured it on the carpet in front of the closet, and then ran the hand vacuum several times over it. There was no rubbing alcohol in the bathroom, so he used a few splashes of cologne, instead. There shouldn't be enough cocaine left for the dog to hit on, and if the dog did indicate, the lab boys would have trouble showing what it was that set him off.

Yorga let himself out and strolled back towards the downtown. As he passed Roosevelt school a second time, he took on more of a shuffle and managed to stumble a time or two, but stayed mostly upright and mostly steady. Unsteady enough to set an impression; not enough to draw attention.

At Lincoln Street, he straightened his step and turned South. He curved his path around the Rotunda and strolled up the steps with purpose. No one challenged him as he walked past the offices of the mayor, the city manager, and the planning commissioners. At the elevator, he took a short ride into the underground garage.

There was a camera at the ramp, and there was a camera on the concrete stairs that led up to the police lot. There was also a camera on the key box itself. The last one was unavoidable.

Yorga entered the override code. The door opened, and each of the sets of keys blinked at him. One by one he withdrew the keys. When he had them all, he walked around the corner, where the garage dead-ended.

He used each set of keys, unlocking the doors and opening the trunks. Then he walked along the rows, closing each trunk lid. When he was done, he locked all of the cars and walked back to the key box. The override code let him put back every set of keys except one.

When he rode the elevator up to the first floor of city hall, he no longer had the plastic bag with the shotgun.

Kojiro walked into the Work Street yard like he owned it. Bentley followed casually behind. Kojiro looked around at the small lot of parked pickups, then marched purposefully towards the maintenance shop. The roll-up door of the first bay was open, and he charged through it. A mechanic was mopping his bay with solvent, and Kojiro marched across the damp cement, leaving boot tracks on the clean floor.

The mechanic looked up at Bentley. "What the hell?" he asked.

Bentley shrugged apologetically, trying to step on Kojiro's footprints. "Not my circus. Not my monkeys," he said. The mechanic gave him a dirty look and mopped over their steps.

The end of the shop featured a hallway, about wide enough for a small car to drive through, with offices on either side. At the end, there was a single door to the outside, and a broad set of steps that went up onto the loft above the right-hand set of offices. Kojiro was quickly pounding his way up those steps when Bentley caught up to him.

"Jenny Mallory?" called Kojiro.

A short woman with a close haircut stepped out from behind a row of storage shelves. She wore a pair of men's work slacks, black boots, and a gray uniform shirt over a black tee-shirt. The left pocket had a white patch that showed her name.

"Yeah?" she said.

"Mind stepping out from behind the counter?"

"Yeah, I mind. I got work to do. You need parts, show me the form. Otherwise, lee-me alone." She started to step back into the shelves.

Bentley grabbed Kojiro's right wrist with his left hand, just as Kojiro started to clear leather.

"What my partner means, Ma'am," said Bentley, loudly, "Is that we are Salinas Police Detectives and we require your assistance in our investigation. We are asking you to step out from behind the counter for our safety."

The woman stepped back into sight. Bentley shoved Kojiro's hand and gun back into the holster. They locked eyes for a moment, then Bentley let go of Kojiro and walked to the end of the counter.

"If you wouldn't mind, Ma'am," he said.

"It's Jenn, not Ma'am," she snapped. But she walked out from the shelves and stood at the end of the counter.

"We have a warrant here," said Bentley. "It says that you need to come downtown with us. We just need to straighten a few things out. It won't take long."

The last two sentences were lies, but everyone on the mezzanine knew that. Still, she let Bentley wave a female officer over for the Terry frisk, and then they all walked slowly down the steps. At the bottom of the steps, Kojiro grabbed Bentley's bicep and pulled him back. The female officer led the suspect out to the waiting transport car.

"What the hell was that?" asked Kojiro. "That was supposed to be my bust."

"I just had a feeling she'd be more comfortable coming with us if we didn't draw our guns."

"Since when are you in charge?"

"I'm not," said Bentley. "You want credit for the arrest, fine with me. But we're not gonna get anywhere shooting suspects before they talk to us. 'Kay?"

Kojiro just glared at him. It didn't bother Bentley. When it came to glaring, Kojiro was a complete amateur. Especially compared to Yorga.

At the suspect's apartment, Kojiro took charge again.

"You want to open the door for us?" he asked.

"No. My keys are in my locker, back at the yard."

Kojiro waved the blue-backed paper at her. "This is a warrant to search these premises," he said. "Don't mess around with us."

She shook her head. "You really want in? I gotta let you in? For real?"

"You have to," said Bentley, apologetically.

"Okay. Bottom of that fire extinguisher, there's a magnet. Magnet's got a key."

Kojiro watched her out of the corner of his eye as he felt the bottom of the extinguisher. He seemed surprised to find the key there, and even more surprised when it worked in the door. He frowned at the officer with the battering ram.

As he pushed the door open, the alarm started to make a series of loud beeps.

"What's the code?" he snapped.

"One…"

"What's the code?" he yelled.

"I'm trine a tell you. One, nine, eight, six."

Kojiro punched one nine eight six, and the alarm stopped beeping. The light on the panel stayed red, but it wasn't beeping.

"Okay," he said. "Bring in the dog."

"You can't do that," said Jenn. "I'm allergic to dogs."

"Stand out in the hallway," snapped Kojiro.

A uniform walked the dog around the apartment. The dog looked up at the handler expectantly. Kojiro scowled. The handler walked around again. Kojiro scowled again, and pointed to the floor by the closet. The handler walked by it again, and the dog obediently sniffed at it, then looked up.

The handler pointed at the closet door. The dog sniffed, and then looked expectantly at the handler. The handler knocked on the door. The dog sniffed it again. Still no indication. The handler shrugged to Kojiro.

Kojiro waved him out of the apartment, and the dog left with his handler.

"Sure this is the right apartment?" asked Bentley.

"This where you live?" snapped Kojiro, looking at the woman.

"Yup," she said.

"Sure she's the right suspect?" asked Bentley, not because he had any doubts, but just to mess with Kojiro.

"Jenny Mallory, City of Salinas employee, works at the Work Street maintenance shop, lives at 3113 Riker, apartment 4. That's where we are."

"Fine by me," shrugged Bentley.

Kojiro yanked open the closet door. "Informant said there was cocaine between two folded blankets in the front closet." He felt between the blankets, and pulled out a pair of mothballs. He said a bad word.

"I don't got any cocaine," said Mallory.

Kojiro walked over to the chair and pulled off the seat cushion. There were a few small coins and a peppermint candy, still wrapped in plastic.

"Somebody's been here," said Kojiro. He turned to Mallory. "Who'd you send over here?"

"What the hell are you talking about?"

"Um, Kojiro … She's been with us this whole time. She didn't have a cell phone, and we haven't let her out of our sight. And we drove straight over here from the city yard." Bentley shrugged yet again. "She didn't call anyone. She couldn't."

"It has to be someone in the city yard, then. They saw us come for her and they called one of her neighbors. We probably just missed them. A few seconds."

"I dunno any of the neighbors," she said. "So, what, you just wanted to feel my blankets and flip over my cushions or something?"

Kojiro felt behind the bookcase, but he already knew that the shotgun wouldn't be there. He shot Bentley a dirty look. "Somebody's leaking information about the investigation," he said.

Bentley wanted to shrug, but he was afraid he'd get a cramp or something. "I wouldn't know," he said. "I just found out we were doing this when we got into the car." He shook his head. "You know, my old partner Yorga, he was a real bonehead sometimes. He got drunk with an informant one time, got the wrong suspect, wrong house, messed up the whole warrant.

"When the search didn't turn up anything – 'cause they were at the wrong house – It blew the whole case. The judge was livid. He told Yorga that if the BAR association came after him, he was gonna throw Yorga under the bus. And make sure it backed up and ran over him again."

Kojiro pursed his lips and turned red in the face.

"I'm not drunk. We have the right informant. It was her partner, Pfalzmann. He gave her up. Pfalzmann faked cutting up the guns, passed them up to her on the mezzanine, and she shipped them as returned parts. We've got her dead to rights."

"How would Pfalzmann know there was cocaine between the blankets in her closet?"

"They were lovers."

The suspect smiled. The suspect tried to hold back, but it was inevitable, unstoppable. The suspect laughed, belly-laughed, roared like a threatened lion, and was completely consumed in irresistible mirth.

Kojiro turned purple and stalked out the door.

When the suspect was finally under control, Bentley offered her his handkerchief. As she dried her eyes and caught her breath, he asked, "I don't suppose that you'd care to make a statement?"

"You told Kojiro that I got drunk with an informant and muffed a warrant?"

"Jones said I was supposed to trash-talk you. It seemed an opportune moment."

"You gonna tell Kojiro later that it never happened?"

"Nah. Who's he gonna tell? And who'd believe him?"

"Okay, well next time make up something a little more believable. Tell him I fell off my pogo stick."

"What did you do with the suspect?"

"Let her go."

"She's really involved, you know."

"Yeah, but unless she confesses, the whole thing's tainted. The faked affidavit for the warrant, the obvious set up – no judge is ever gonna buy that. She'd walk at arraignment."

"He's probably coming after you next."

"No chance. He still thinks I'm just a big dumb cop."

"Yeah, well, that's silly. You're not that big."

Yorga got up and walked to the stove, where an old-fashioned percolator was chugging away. He turned off the fire and held it out towards Bentley. Bentley shook his head, so Yorga only refilled his own mug.

"So how was Jenn Mallory related to you again?"

"She's not really. She's an old friend of Mauri, my ex-girlfriend."

"I know who Mauri was." The wry look on Bentley's face suggested he'd have preferred not to know.

"She lent us her apartment a couple of times. Which was a little weird, but that was before I knew everything about Mauri."

"I wish I knew less about her."

"Anyway, Herb told me that there were three people he thought might be involved. Jenn was one of them. So the next one that they rolled up would have to be one of those three." He sniffed the cream and decided against it.

"What tipped you that it would be her, and today?"

"I found out that the warrant was being signed, and that was that. Jenn might or might not be dirty, but nobody deserves to be framed." He seated himself across the wooden table from Bentley.

"Nobody's gonna notice lights on in here?"

"Well, I'm careful to keep the lights low and the shades drawn, first of all," said Yorga. "And I walked around the house last night, about fifty yards out. Trees and sheds block any view from the main road, there's that ridge to the east, and there's a row of eucalyptus to the north. Somebody would have to suspect that I was here."

"And you're not gonna go take in a ball game this time, right?"

Yorga shrugged. "It was stupid, but I was goin' stir-crazy at Earl's place. You'd a hated it. Nothing to read, no books, not even a newspaper. Just TV."

"So now," said Bentley, "The next question is what to do about that." He gestured to the cellophane-wrapped package of cocaine on Herb's table.

"We can't put it back into the evidence locker," said Yorga. "It's tainted."

"We don't even know what case it came from. Originally, I mean. So that means that somewhere, a drug dealer walks."

"Naw," dismissed Yorga. "The DA's good at plea-bargains. I mean, if you know they seized a kilo of coke from your trunk, are you really gonna argue that you didn't know it was there?"

"Okay, yeah, the actual evidence will be irrelevant. Which is why they had the liberty to use it in the case against Pfalzmann, and then in the case against you."

"Which means that someone with easy access to the property room is dirty."

"Kojiro came out of property. Then they gave him a gold shield for no apparent reason."

"And we know he's dirty."

"So what do we do with it?"

"Well," sighed Yorga, sipping Herb's coffee. "I can't just hold onto it. It's a toxic hot potato."

"So if we should arrange for Kojiro to recover it somehow…"

"Yeah, and then it gets put into an evidence bag at my trial. Not exactly a good plan. As it is, they have to find another kilo somewhere before Herb goes to trial, and the more things they do, the more chance there is they'll be caught."

"So far they've been pretty blatant and they've still gotten away with it. If Herb hadn't blown the whistle…"

"I have an idea," said Bentley. "But we might need a little bit of time to set it up."

"On the top shelf, left side of the cabinets." replied Yorga. "Between tarragon and tumeric."

Bentley glared at him. Then they both grinned.

"I missed the repartee," said Bentley. "Kojiro's a cold fish. No sense of humor at all. It seems to have been replaced with a sense of entitlement."

"They'll be coming for you soon enough."

"Even with Kojiro's magic algorithm that says I'm clean as a nun's laundry?"

"They'll decide they didn't carry the three, and oops, you're dirty after all."

"Coke in the closet?"

"They're so lazy, they'd probably use the same bag if they still had it."

"I thought you were paranoid, putting in the second set of cameras at your apartment."

"Well, I probably was. But a bit of paranoia can be healthy when they really are out to get you."

"So what are my options?"

"Isn't there some book people use when they declare war?" asked Yorga. "People always talk about some kind of art thing."

"You mean Sun Tzu, no doubt," said Bentley. "*The Art of War*. It's a classic."

"Any good?"

"If you want to teach the emperor's concubines how to march in formation, it's priceless. But I lean more towards the *Go Rin No Sho*, by Miyamoto Mushashi."

"Anything useful in it?"

"You may use a strategy once, or perhaps twice, but never a third time. That's pretty useful. And do not become attached to earthly things. Also, he said to always be thinking of how you may cut the enemy."

"I suppose that's mildly useful. Still, I was hoping for more practical advice – tactics we might be able to use."

"You know that one guy in traffic that lifts all the weights at the gym?"

"The guy that's always bragging about his guns?"

"The one that always kisses his biceps and says, 'These ain't just guns, fellas. These are naval ordnance.' You know."

"Yeah, that guy, okay. And sometimes he says, 'Abs like these ought to be illegal.' "

"That would be a navel ordinance. Well, he's always reciting something called the *Dictum Boelke*. Advice from one fighter pilot to another, back in World War 1. Things like, always attack from out of the sun, always have an advantage of altitude, check for additional planes before diving on an enemy."

"If I can lure them into the air, I'll try to use that."

"Boelke got shot down. So did his student, the bloody Baron von Richtoffen. So maybe it's not the whole story. There might be some better advice out there somewhere."

"So we're plowing completely fresh ground here, is that what you're telling me?"

"Seems that way." Bentley put his coffee cup on the table and stared at it for a moment.

"Well, when they come for you – and they will – We can do the same thing we did with Jenn. The evidence isn't there. Or… some of the evidence isn't there."

"And I go sit with Herb in the County lockup?"

"Or you do like I did and catch a train."

"They'll be watching the station this time. You caught them off-guard because they didn't think you'd dump your car with a major highway so close at hand."

"And I escaped San Diego because they thought I'd stick to trains. These guys don't seem to have much of a third dimension."

"We'd still better not underestimate them. I drove all the way to Soledad before doubling back and coming here. On the way home, I'll take a long tour through Prunedale. Just in case they've begun tracking my car's daily mileage."

"If they put you on GPS, we're in trouble. We'd better meet in town next time. You could say you stopped for a *torta de jamon.*"

"Or even a ham sandwich." Bentley took one last gulp of coffee and started out the door.

Chapter Eight

KOJIRO WAS LATE, as usual. He marched into the squad room as if it was everybody else's fault that he was late, scowling at the other detectives who, for the most part, never noticed.

He pulled open the lower drawer of his desk, looked inside, and then turned to Bentley, who was intently reading a file folder that lay open in front of him. He looked back into the drawer, stared for a moment, then looked back at Bentley.

"Anybody mess with my desk this morning?"

Bentley looked up from the folder. "Just you, as far as I saw. Why? Something wrong?"

"Nothing," said Kojiro. "Must've been someone's idea of a practical joke."

Bentley knew what was bothering Kojiro. He'd been visited by the nose-powder fairy, and he was wondering how a kilogram of the white stuff had found its way into his desk. And also how it had coincidentally appeared in the very same drawer that held unsealed evidence bags, marked with the case numbers for Herb Pfalzmann and Franz Yorga.

Kojiro waited until Bentley went back to his file folder before carefully locking his desk drawers. He wasn't sure how to report this, or even if he needed … Well, Xeng would go crazy if he didn't. Either way, actually. Might as well get it over with.

He gave the room a discreet glance and then headed off to find a private spot for a phone call.

In the Santa Clara warehouse, the atmosphere was thick with tension. Louis Xeng was very angry, and he wasn't shy about letting it be known.

"Who'd you send to set up the Mallory woman?" snapped Xeng, glaring at Chuck.

"Local talent," said Chuck. "Nobody important."

"He messed it up. Didn't plant the evidence, then somehow got the cocaine into Yoshi's desk drawer."

"That's mighty bold."

"Too bold, and too incompetent. You find out what he did, and if he maybe did the wrong apartment."

"He reported it done."

"It wasn't done. The coke wasn't there." Xeng shook his head. "Don't pay him."

"Too late."

"Too late? You paid him already for this?"

Chuck shrugged. "He reported it done, and he's always been reliable before."

Xeng made a noise that was between a sigh and a growl. "You find out what went wrong. And you don't use him again." Xeng stared at Chuck for a moment.

"Next time, you do the job yourself. And you wait around until the police arrive."

"I gotta go to Salinas?" groused Chuck. Xeng silenced him with a stare.

Bentley wove his car through a maze of small pseudo-Spanish-style buildings next to Natividad Medical Center. He parked in a narrow parking lot next to a building marked "Danger: Keep out." Bentley did exactly that, keeping out of the large condemned physical plant building.

Instead, he knocked on the door of the low glass-and-aluminum building across from it. A small woman peered through a window in the door, then pushed it open slightly.

"May I help you?"

"Detective Bentley, here to see Kim King."

She opened the door and let him in, closing it behind him. "King's in his office," she said. "But I'll need you to sign in first." She pointed to a three-ring binder open on the counter.

"In that case, is there any chance he could come meet me out here in your foyer?"

"You'll still have to sign in," she said.

Bentley reluctantly allowed his presence to be recorded and time-stamped, then followed the indicated hallway to the office at the end. King was there, finishing a salami sandwich.

"You don't leave for lunch?" asked Bentley, instead of offering a greeting.

"Nope. I have the secretary bring me something. I can never decide. I just tell her to surprise me. What can I do for you? Here to arrest me?"

"Have you committed any crimes?"

"Not recently, but according to the internet, that never stops a good arrest. Did you ever find the guy that was shooting at the governor that time? He broke two of my windows."

"I actually came to ask for some help."

"Oh, cool. You need to see our security video from the ER ambulance bay? Looking for a fugitive who was maybe wounded escaping? Something like that? Want some chips?"

Bentley wished, not for the first time, that King had a speed control of some kind, to slow his speech and his train of thought to normal human standard.

"I need to know if you can help me with some electronics. I need them modified." He pulled out a pair of devices, shrink-wrapped to rigid cardstock. "I need these to be at about 30,000 hertz, and well over 120 db."

"30,000? That's kind of specific. Nothing below 20,000, eh?"

"But very, very, loud. Painful."

"Might have to raise the voltage a little, and it might not fit in this case. That okay?"

"As long as it works the way it works now."

"You got it."

"How soon can you do it?"

"Got some time? We can step into the shop right now. Take me maybe twenty, twenty-five minutes?"

"One other favor. Don't tell anybody about it."

King stopped and gave him a pained look. "That takes all the fun out of it."

"Okay, silence for now. In three months, you can tell anybody you want, and I'll even tell you why."

"Where you been?" asked Kojiro, when Bentley got back to the station. "We've got a search warrant."

"Somebody else hiding mothballs in their sheets?"

"That woman tipped someone off."

"Yeah, just ribbin' you. Who are we searching?"

"Gonzales Helvetic Gun Club," said Kojiro, with a smile. "Two of our suspects are members there, so we're gonna open their lockers and see what they got. Maybe look around a little while we're there."

"Why don't we just declare war on the whole South County?"

"You don't think we should follow up leads?"

"Don't mind me," said Bentley. "I'm just running my mouth. Lead on."

The Gonzales Helvetic Gun Club proved to be a good drive out of Gonzales, near the Santa Lucia mountains. An oak-lined hillside provided wide picnic grounds, with a slope that started near flat and increased slowly nearer the mountains.

The mountains themselves provided a natural backdrop for the shooting ranges, flat patches carved from the earth with tall berms built up on all sides. Subtle furrows denoted the shooting stations: paths out two or three hundred yards, worn down by endless shooters posting, checking, and removing targets.

"A reverse lead mine," said Bentley, pointing. Kojiro stared at him. "Yeah, never mind."

The two detectives let themselves into the offices and approached the formica counter. A tall man in his mid-thirties stood up from a desk and walked over to them. He was casually dressed, in that he wore a simple western shirt with blue jeans and a large metal buckle, but there was nothing casual about his outfit or his demeanor. The line of his buttons exactly met the center of the belt buckle. The shirt, the jeans, and the expensive alligator cowboy boots were all crisp and sharp. Despite the open collar, he could not have been more precisely dressed had he worn a suit.

"Can I help you, Gentlemen?" he asked, in a flat, professional tone that was both inquiry and challenge.

"Search warrant," said Kojiro.

"We're police detectives on the combined task force," clarified Bentley. He produced his ID and held it in front of him.

The crisp cowboy held out a hand for it, and allowed Bentley to give it to him. Then he looked at Kojiro.

Kojiro returned the stare. Bentley nudged him. Shooting a glare at Bentley, Kojiro produced his ID and handed it to the cowboy at the counter.

The cowboy stared at Bentley's ID, then Kojiro's. He took his time, reading the details and matching the picture to the faces. Then he wrote down the names and badge numbers on a small white pad of paper. He held out both IDs. Bentley accepted them, handing one to Kojiro.

"You said something about a warrant?"

Kojiro pulled the warrant from an inside pocket and slapped it onto the counter. The cowboy, with measured coolness, unfolded the paper and read it carefully.

"Please wait here, Gentlemen," he said, turning and walking into a small office. Kojiro started to follow, but Bentley grasped his bicep firmly.

"He'll be back," said Bentley. "He's not fleeing the interview."

Bentley looked around the large room. It was a bit like a hotel lobby. There were comfortable chairs and sofas in conversational groupings. It was also a bit like a golf course pro shop, except that instead of golf clubs and golf balls, it offered targets, leather holsters, cleaning supplies, and gun-related merchandise.

A shorter Hispanic man came out of the office. He was wearing jeans and a button-down shirt, open at the collar, with a vest over it. As with the first man, he appeared formally casual.

"Gentlemen," he said, offering the warrant back to them. "I understand that you are here to see some of the lockers of our members?"

"We have a warrant," said Bentley, "For the lockers of Herb Pfalzmann and Franz Yorga."

"Ah," said the man in the vest. "I will not be able to assist you with the latter request. Mr. Yorga is an associate member, and does not have an assigned locker."

"Associate member?" asked Bentley. "So Mr. Pfalzmann is a full member, and has a locker?"

"Yes. But Mr. Yorga is not actually Swiss, and does not qualify for full membership."

"Are you a member?" asked Kojiro.

"Yes, a full member."

"You don't look very Swiss."

"My people come from the Spanish-Swiss region, where the border of Switzerland meets Spain."

Bentley grinned, but managed to hide it by swiping his hand over his face. Kojiro just tilted his head. He wasn't entirely sure, but he thought maybe the man had just called him an idiot.

"Okay," said Kojiro. "Let's get this over with."

"Sorry," said Bentley, "But what was your name?"

"Tomas Miguel," he said, with a nod of his head. "I am the club's legal counsel." Miguel motioned towards a door in the back of the room.

The room he led them into held several rows of lockers, all of them full-sized. He casually glanced at the doors, one by one, until he found a certain locker. There was a small padlock dangling from the latch, but the shackle was open.

"Somebody already been here, messing with this locker?" asked Kojiro, staring at Miguel.

"Mr. Pfalzmann usually doesn't keep much in his locker," said Miguel. "I would assume that between that fact, and the fact that he trusts the overall security of the club beyond any question, he sees no reason to lock up."

Bentley unhooked the lock from the latch and pulled the door open. There was a small paper bag in the bottom of the locker. It was otherwise empty. Bentley picked up the bag.

"Empty .22 rimfire shells," said Bentley.

"Bag it and tag it," said Kojiro. "I bet the firing pin marks match the stolen gun in his house."

Kojiro walked over to a small closet and yanked the door open. It was full of mops and cleaning supplies.

"Excuse me," said Miguel. "I believe that your warrant covers the locker, not the cleaning closet."

"You have some secrets hidden away in that closet?"

"Of course not," said Miguel. "But you have no right at all to examine it. And as the old adage goes, rights undefended are lost forever. Thus, if you gentlemen are done, I will have to ask you to leave at once."

Kojiro looked around the room. With there being only one locker, and it nearly empty, there was nothing else to do. Reluctantly, he allowed himself to be herded out of the locker room alongside Bentley.

Chapter Nine

SINCE THIS ODD affair began, Bentley had developed a daily routine. On rising in the morning, he would carefully check his towels and blankets to make sure that there wasn't a kilo of cocaine hidden between them in his closets. He would then look around his apartment for guns that weren't there.

Having found no contraband, he would look at his security camera, wave politely, and then let himself out the door. A tiny slip of paper wedged into the door jam would serve as a warning if the door were opened before he returned.

Then, and only then, he would make his way down to his car to go to work. This particular day, two men were in the underground garage, standing in front of his car, as if judging it for a car show.

"Can I help you?" he asked, resting his hand on the pistol hidden in the discreet holster on his hip.

The two men turned around, and Bentley recognized them. One of them was a Saturday Night Cowboy, with boots, straight-leg jeans, and a button-down with faux-pearl snaps instead of buttons. The other was a short slightly-round Hispanic man in his fifties. The latter wore a crisp dark gray suit with a thin black tie.

The Hispanic man spoke. "I am Tomas Miguel. My associate is Mr. Crenshaw. We met yesterday, at the …"

"From the Gonzales Helvetic Firearm Society. Of course." Bentley nodded. "And how might I help you?"

"I will be speaking to Mr. Pfalzmann today, to see if he needs representation. And assuming that his interests parallel those of Mr. Pfalzmann, I will likewise offer my services to Franz Yorga."

"Good to know," said Bentley. "But this is an unusual venue for a counsel notification."

"I am not in touch with Franz. I was hoping you might convey the offer of counsel."

"I notice he's Franz, and Herb is Mr. Pfalzmann. Should I assume that Yorga's in better standing with the club?"

"Let's say that the organization owes a debt of gratitude to your former partner."

"Which is why he's an associate member, even though he's a Czech?"

"Being Swiss is a state of mind, Mr. Bentley. I, myself, am less than perfectly qualified. But as our founder, Koji Yamamoto, was fond of saying, to be Swiss in one's soul is to be Swiss in one's genes as well."

"Yamamoto?"

"No relation to the famous admiral, before you ask. In Japan, the name Yamamoto is as common as Johnson to an American."

"So you want to know if I can get a message to Yorga for you, is that it?"

"It seems likely that our interests run in parallel."

"Alright, I can acknowledge that our interests are somewhat similar."

"But of course, if you were in touch with Franz, you would not be able to convey our offer. Because of, you understand, where you stand, in relation to the situation in which we find ourselves."

Bentley nodded, partly in admiration of the man's talent for circumlocution. If there were any doubt that Miguel was a lawyer, that would have settled it.

"True," said Bentley. "In that hypothetical situation, I'd be guilty of harboring a fugitive. A felony, you understand."

"We would certainly not wish to place such a blot on your escutcheon."

"Nor such a stain on my record, no doubt."

"So we will fully understand if you cannot indicate whether Franz has received our message."

"Perhaps he will get in touch with you himself, without any help from me."

"A consummation devoutly to be wished." the two men walked away, leaving Bentley standing. He watched them climb into an immaculate old Ford pickup truck. Early 70s, by the grill, but clean and shiny as if it were made yesterday. As they drove away, he glanced at his watch. Just enough time to get doughnuts and make it to work on time.

Do you trust Tomas Miguel? asked the text message.

Yorga thought for a moment. *Tomas Miguel from the Gonzales Helvetic Firearm Club?*

He wants to offer his services in your defense.

Well, that was nice of him. Yorga thought about it for a moment. *He might not like our plan.*

He doesn't need to know, came the reply.

Maybe we should wait until we need him.

Call him.

Yorga put down the phone and opened Herb's fridge. The milk was going blinky, the eggs had an odd hollow feel to them, and the cheese was growing a grayish-blue fur. Not that he would have gone for the cheese, anyway. He had a faint suspicion that it was Limburger.

Still, an omelet was out of the question. Coffee was possible, and Herb's taste in coffee beans at least made a potable brew, but Yorga was going to need some groceries. He tore a page from the pad glued to the refrigerator door and looked around for a pencil.

Out the window over the kitchen sink, motion caught his eye. He looked across the fields, where a single yellow pickup drew to a stop. It was at least half a mile away, but Yorga took a half-step back from the window. It would not do to be seen.

There was a logo on the door of the truck. Yorga thought he could make out white writing below the logo. The driver rolled down his window and stuck out his head. Then, after an interminably long moment, he rolled up the window and drove away, bouncing unevenly through the field roads. Yorga watched until he was completely gone from view.

Yorga sighed. Going to the market was out of the question. Maybe a diet was in order. He searched the shelves again and found a small bag of pinto beans. The magical fruit…

Aron Salazar shook his head. It was probably a trick of the light, or a reflection in the window. Or maybe old Herb got himself a house cat. Maybe he should call somebody and let 'em know.

He'd look into it when he was done with the pumps.

For now, there was a pump shed with a flashing red light near the Airline Highway. One of the irrigation pumps was having trouble. And when he was done with that, there was a pump to check out over in field 93 west.

Aron gave the truck a little gas … very little, because there was a fine line between moving quickly through the muddy fields and getting stuck in a row of brussells sprouts. The truck bounced along through the shallow ruts of the narrow margin between the fields.

By the time he was pulling up to the pump shed, the odd reflection in Herb's window was almost completely forgotten.

"They had to let her go," said Kojiro.

Bentley mulled that in his brain for a moment before realizing that the "her" was Jenn Mallory. "So the search was a bust, eh?"

"Didn't find a single thing. And her lawyer came in breathing fire. No just cause for the warrant, improper affidavit, happiest corpses, blah blah blah."

Bentley was tempted to pat him on the shoulder and cheer him up by promising not to call a lawyer when it was his turn, but he couldn't bring himself to do it. Besides, the schadenfreude was just too sweet. Instead, he opened the pink pasteboard box in his hand and held it towards Kojiro.

"Have a doughnut," offered Bentley.

"Things'll kill ya," said Kojiro, looking at Bentley as if he had offered him a water moccasin.

"I got an appointment this morning," said Bentley. "Might take a couple hours. Just so you know." He put the box on an unused desk in the squad room, retrieved a cruller from the box, and let himself out.

Bentley's appointment was actually a bit of research time. He spent a fair while reviewing old cases involving the Gonzales Helvetic Firearms Club. Gonzales PD had been called out once, for a minor altercation at an event. It was a group renting the facility for a picnic, and not members themselves, so it really didn't matter for Bentley's purposes.

A similar check of Tomas Miguel revealed that he had an excellent reputation and was well-respected among his peers, both in the legal community and the Hispanic community as well. And it looked like he got along pretty nicely with the local Swiss.

Crenshaw was a bit of a cipher. Still, lack of notoriety tended to be a good sign. In all, as background checks went, the two men and the organization they represented seemed clean.

Bentley wondered if that was because they were, in fact, every bit as innocent as they seemed, or because they had carefully scrubbed the records. Was that possibly the great favor which left them indebted to Yorga?

Nonsense. If Yorga wasn't dirty, then he wasn't doing any favors for people who were. Still, one thing about the Helvetic Gun Society rankled with Bentley. It was a case about guns, and they had a strong interest in guns. Too much coincidence.

So were they involved, and if so, on what side?

"Hugh are new in town, eh?"

Yorga looked the cashier in the eye. He said nothing.

"I see you around a little bit, last week or so. *Mira*, we got good weekly deals. You buy here, we can get you discounts, you know? This week, tomorrow, I got *pollo preparado*, ready for the barbeque. All boneless thigh, special marinade we make in the back. Three pounds, only ten dollars."

"Not a bad deal," conceded Yorga. "I'll see how the missus feels about it." It made him a bit worried that he was turning into a public figure around a very small town. Making up a wife might throw the local narrative a little off track.

"*Ah, si, mi amigo.* They make all the decisions, right? Still, she send you, maybe you bring back what you want, tell her we don't got what she want. I back you up." He looked around, in case Yorga's *esposa* was lurking in one of the aisles. "We got *cerveza barrata*, real good, but cheap."

"Thanks," said Yorga. "None today, but maybe I'll want some for this weekend." He picked up his paper bags and let himself out of the store.

Once again, he wasn't as invisible as he thought. At least he hadn't driven Herb's pickup into town. Not that banging around in Herb's dusty old Coronet made much of a difference: If anyone knew the car they'd know he was staying out at Herb's.

The provisions in the bags would let him stay hidden on the farm for a little while, at least. If it went very much longer, he could maybe have Bentley make deliveries.

Or maybe he'd have to take a bigger risk and start grocery-shopping in Gonzales, fifteen minutes south of Chualar. But it was that kind of reasoning that had screwed up a good hiding place in San Diego, wasn't it?

Keeping a low profile isn't as easy as it seems, he decided. No more trips to town.

Jenn Mallory was as nervous as a prom queen in a liquor store with a fake ID. The deputy was nonchalant as he took her visitor card and pointed down the row of concrete booths.

Each concrete booth had maybe a foot and a half of privacy wall between it and the next booth. Each featured a tiny shelf, maybe six inches wide, and a perfectly-round stainless steel seat on a post, bolted securely to the floor. Above the tiny shelf, there was a large window, made of glass with a wire grid sandwiched between the thick layers.

Jenn noted that all the screws around the metal frame were on her side. She supposed it made sense. It wasn't impossible that someone on the inside might get a T-30H bit, for security screws like these, and something to turn it with. Or manage to improvise something. Folks were real clever sometimes.

She got to the second to last window, and there was Herb, sitting patiently on a stool like the one in front of her. She sat down and picked up the handset on the wall. Herb picked up his as well.

"Herb?" she asked.

"Who else is it gonna be?" he snapped, as his voice, tinny and crackling, came through the handset.

"Yeah," she said. "Lissen, you been talkin' to people about me? You tell somebody I had cocaine? 'Cause you know that ain't me. I don't do that stuff."

"I don't say nothing to anybody about anything," said Herb. "I got no idea why I'm in here."

"You dint make up nothin' about us bein' lovers? Nothin' like that? 'Cause there's rumors."

"About me and you? They crazy out there?" He shook his head. "Look, Jenn, I got nothin' against you, we worked together for a long time. But, you know…"

"Yeah, you ain't my type. But somebody said that, and the police busted into my apartment lookin' for cocaine. Arrested me at work, too. In front of the whole shop."

"Who was it? The cop with the sleeves too long?"

"Yeah, but the one leadin' things was a Asian guy."

"Not a big guy with a tweed jacket?"

"Yorga? No, this guy was smaller."

"They find any cocaine?"

"No, I dint have none. But they was so sure they was gonna find it. Even said where it was spos'd to be, in my closet, between two blankets. Like somebody told 'em something."

"I never been to your apartment. Wouldn't know where you keep anything. And irregardless, I'm just sittin' in here keepin' my mouth shut and my back to the wall. Because somebody's up to somethin' out there."

"Okay, look, this stuff somebody's sayin' about me, I gotta know. They said it was you saying it, so I gotta ask. You know."

"Can't blame you. I'd ask too."

"Hey, you need anything? Anything I can do since you're in here? You know, to make up, accusing you of talkin' trash?"

"If you wanted to swing by my place and make sure there aren't squatters in the barn, that'd be nice. But don't make a special trip. No, honest, it was good to get off the pod for a few."

"Take care, Herb."

She hung up the phone and walked back down the narrow row. Two other booths were in use, one a young woman with a baby who was talking to a thick man with a blond buzzcut and a goatee. He shot a glare at Jenn as she walked by.

She nodded to the corrections officer, who made a note on her card and then opened the door for her. Stepping out into the open air gave her a sense of relief. She had gone into the lion's den and walked out with no tooth marks.

When she was a little ways down the path, the corrections officer stepped into a small cubicle and picked up a phone. "Sarge," he said, "You're gonna wanna run the tape on booth five just now."

Aron Salazar found himself looking at Herb's house whenever he drove through the fields. Maybe it looked a little bit like the curtains had been moved a little. Maybe not. Who could say, from this distance?

Hard to tell. He wondered if he should start taking pictures on his cell phone. So he could compare, day to day. In case something moved. No, that would be a little weird. A lot weird.

Probably nothing to worry about. That one reflection that he thought he saw the one time… that might have been the sun, making the glass sparkle, or maybe it was just his imagination.

Was it worthwhile to drive over and check it out?

He'd feel kinda stupid if it turned out nobody was there. Or if it was somebody Herb sent to take care of things. Or if it was cops.

Yeah, the cops spent a lot of time messing around over there, after Herb got arrested. Maybe they were still going through the place sometimes. Aron wasn't very comfortable with cops.

Maybe it was best if Aron minded his own business.

Aron nodded to himself. Mind his own business, that was the best thing he could do. Still, it hung in the back of his mind.

Jenn Mallory sat in her best chair, the one that jackass had searched. Why was he so sure that she would have a gun here? Or that she kept cocaine between her blankets? And most puzzling of all, where the hell did the mothballs come from?

She could understand that the cops might screw up and think she was dirty. She could even understand what made 'em suspect her. She'd been afraid for years that there someone might go looking for parts on her day off and open the wrong box.

But the cocaine? No, never in a million years. She wasn't stupid. If she was dealing in something like that, no way in hell would she make it so traceable to her. No merchandise ever came to her apartment; it was always at the shop, on the mezzanine, where she could blame it on someone else. Taking it home? No, that would be stupid.

The inventory she did have... The unmarked boxes in the warehouse... Well, she needed to offload that, and quick. But that was probably what they expected. They'd be watching, and they'd probably tap her phones. She watched all the cop shows, and she knew how they put stuff in your phones, and cloned your cell, and all that.

Well, that made it simple. She'd get a burner cell, and she'd work out a way for the unmarked boxes to find their way to Louis. And then she'd tell Louis she was out, laying low for a while.

Maybe she'd take some time off, head down to Brawley, see what Mauri was up to. Mauri would be surprised to see her. Wait, didn't she move some place in Arizona? Yeah, Kingman, that was it. Even better. It was out of state.

On the drive down, she could stop in Chualar, swing by Herb's place, make sure nobody was livin' in his barn. Not that it was likely, but you never knew.

Still, one thing bothered her: The mothballs. Without those ... no, it was pretty clear: somebody had been in her place. Somebody that knew about the key under the extinguisher. And until the raid, that was a short list.

Chapter Ten

YORGA WAS SITTING in Herb's very best chair, nodding off to sleep with an Ed McBain novel on his chest, when a flash of light brought him to full alert. There it was again, on the glass over the face of the grandfather clock. Something outside had reflected a beam of light through one of the windows, making a momentary glimmer. Something outside was moving. Something shiny.

Yorga drew his off-duty piece and slipped quickly over to the front wall. He stood beside the picture window and carefully peered past the edge of the curtain, careful not to move it. After a breathless second, he caught it again. A single car, moving slowly up the dirt road from town.

The evening sun had caught the windshield just right, flashing a beacon his way. Good thing he hadn't nodded off. He glanced at the bullet hole over the chair he had been sitting in. If it was that trigger-happy Kojiro, that nap could have been the end of him.

He slipped through the house, letting himself out the kitchen door, away from the car. He retreated to one of the sheds. It was two-sided, like a chevron, with only a bare post to support the roof at the fourth corner. He took up a position in the dark shadows behind an ancient Allis-Chalmers tractor.

Bentley pulled the car around between two sheds, where it would be as hidden as possible, and waited a moment for the following cloud of dust to settle and to drift on by him. Then he got out, popped the trunk, and lifted out a large cardboard box.

He was just setting it down on the step when he heard a voice behind him.

"You couldn't have called, to let me know you were coming?"

"I'm trying to be discreet," he replied, as Yorga walked past him and opened the door. "Plus the cell coverage is a little spotty out here." He picked up the box and followed Yorga to the kitchen.

"I figured you were probably running low on provisions, so I brought you a few things."

"Nice of you."

"Hope you like tomato soup. Walmart had a special."

"I picked up a few provisions in town, but it's probably best if I don't go back for a while. Guy in the store recognized me."

"He knows you?"

"No, but he said he's seen me around town. Tried to sell me cheap beer and marinated chicken thighs."

"Take in a Padres game while you were out?"

"No, and I get the point. I'm laying low."

"Well, I also got you some vegetables. I figured this might be a good time to start a healthy diet. For snacking, I got you a case of protein bars."

"Those things aren't very nice. I tried one once. It tasted like baked sawdust."

"It's reconstituted soy lecithin and plant-based proteins. It's good for you."

"A good steak is what's good for me. Speaking of which, I was gonna fire up Herb's grill and cook some hanger steak that I got down at *Quatro Hermanos*. You wanna stay for dinner?"

"What the hell. I've got no plans. You know, they've got fake-steak, too. It's made from cashews and walnuts, mostly, with a sesame-oil binder. Tastes like real meat. It even sizzles when you fry it in a pan."

"You know, I found an old family recipe for making plants taste just like meat. You know what it is? You feed it to a cow. Works great. And you'd never know it's not real beef. Because it is."

Aron Salazar was a long way away, and the sun was partly in his eyes, but he was pretty sure that he saw someone slip out the door of Herb's house and hide in the shed. And now, it looked like there might be a light in the kitchen.

Could be some friends of Herb's taking care of the place. Or maybe Herb was back. Or maybe somebody was staying in Herb's old place; someone who shouldn't be in there. Squatters, or somebody taking advantage.

Aron was not going to walk up and knock on the door. If it was bad guys, he could get shot. And if it was, like, family; they'd be pretty mad. Like he was sticking his nose into things where he didn't belong.

Maybe he should just call somebody. Yeah. That was probably the best thing. Just call somebody, and let them worry about it.

With that settled, he turned his attention to the road and drove home.

"Not a bad steak," said Bentley. "Grills up nicely."

"They normally marinate it in the store," said Yorga, "But they had a nice fresh one, and hadn't put it in yet, so I asked for it without the marinade. The butcher looked at me like I was *loco*, but he sold it that way."

"Good call. And the leftovers will give you something to chew on besides the case."

"What's the word on that?"

"Well, they couldn't hold Jenn Mallory, you probably figured that. And me and Kojiro got a good look around at the Helvetic Gun Club."

"I don't figure that you saw much to excite curiosity. Why drag them into this?"

"You and Herb are both members, him full and you partial, and they have guns."

"Can't beat logic like that. Hey, we both live in California, and we both drive cars. Wow, you know what? Jenn does, too! You should go to Sacramento and raid the DMV building."

"Jenn really is in on the gun thing, isn't she?"

"Not exactly. I've been investigating…"

"Quiet," said Bently, flicking off the kitchen light. Yorga turned around and saw the cause of Bentley's concern. A pair of headlights was making its way down the small rise, along the dirt road. Yorga drew his off-duty revolver and stood up in the dark.

"You stay here, cover the front," said Yorga. "I'll slip out the side and get behind them."

Bentley watched the way the lights bounced along the ruts. It was clearly a pickup truck, from the way it moved. That was a good sign; it ruled out law enforcement. They'd be in Dodge Chargers and Ford Crown Victorias. But it didn't rule out the bad guys.

It seemed to take forever for the pickup to drift along the road, before it finally turned into the open patch of ground between the sheds and the house. The headlights cut off suddenly.

It was too dark for Yorga to tell how many people were in the truck, or who it was. The doors did not open. No one made any attempt to get out. It was as if they were debating what to do next, or possibly just waiting for Yorga to notice them.

Without warning, the headlights began to flash on and off. It had been a long time since Yorga had read Morse code, but he got the general idea: F-R-A-N-Z -- D-O-N-T -- S-H-O-O-T.

There was another pause, in total darkness, then the message repeated again. The front porch light came on and went off again. Bentley, acknowledging the message.

After a slight pause, the headlights flashed out a new message: I-T-S -- T-O-M-A-S.

Yorga holstered his gun. Bentley let the message repeat again before acknowledging it, as before. But Yorga was already moving, in the dark, around to the driver's door of the truck. He knocked on the glass with his knuckles.

There was a choking sound inside the truck, then the window rolled down. "You startled me," said Tomas Miguel. "I thought you were still in the house."

"I have friends," said Yorga. "Are you alone?"

"Just me. I thought it best this way."

"Are you armed?"

"I am merely a lawyer, Franz," he answered, with distinct disappointment in his voice. "My only weapon is a subpoena."

"Got one in there?"

"None at all. Not so much as a waiver of liability."

"Why don't we go inside?"

"Mr. Bentley will not shoot us?"

"No, he's good about choosing his targets." Yorga turned to the house as Miguel stepped out of the truck. "Code 4," he said, loudly. Bentley flicked on the porch light and left it on.

"Mister Miguel," said Bentley, through the closed screen door. "Nice to see you again."

"Likewise," said the lawyer, as he stepped onto the porch. "I'm glad that you're here; it will simplify matters significantly."

"We just finished dinner," said Yorga. "The grill's not hot, but I can rewarm the steak in the oven."

"Gracious of you," said Miguel. "But I've already eaten. Perhaps we might have a word or two about the more pressing matter before us?"

Yorga motioned him to a chair at the table. "Coffee?" he asked, as Bentley reseated himself.

"A cup would be nice," said Miguel. "No sugar, but perhaps a slight splash of milk."

"No milk," said Yorga.

"I brought you some powdered creamer," said Bentley. "It's in the box with the soup."

"Ah," said Miguel. "So that answers one of my questions, namely, how you were being provisioned. The kindness of friends."

"How did you know I was here?" asked Yorga, pouring the coffee into three cups. He opened the creamer and offered it to Miguel, who shook a little into his coffee.

"Partly deduction, and partly observation," he replied. "With no small part of guesswork. But I am confident that you are safe here, at least for now." He sipped the coffee. "Did Mr. Bentley tell you of my offer?"

"To represent me?"

"Yes. *Pro bono,* if you will allow it."

"I'd be honored."

"Well, there is one small item we must agree upon up front. None of us are here. You, Franz, did not break into a suspect's home and take up residence there. And you, Mr. Bentley —"

"Byron, please."

"You, Byron, did not knowingly give aid and comfort to a fugitive from justice. And I have no idea where you are, Franz, as it would be my duty to persuade you to surrender to the police."

"Canons and all that," said Bentley.

"Like the 1812 overture," said Miguel.

"Agreed," said Yorga.

"Likewise," said Bentley.

"And I as well," said Miguel. "With that settled, might we discuss the matter at hand?"

"The floor is yours," said Bentley.

"So," said Tomas Miguel, "as you can imagine, it is difficult to maintain an organization such as this. I refer to the Helvetic Gun Club, of course. In particular, there is the question of membership. It is our rule that a full member must have at least one Swiss great-grandparent, must be sponsored by a member, and must have good moral character.

"This last characteristic is left slightly ambiguous, you understand. There are legal precedents that would protect our right to freely choose our membership, but there are also legal precedents which would deny us that right. So we maintain the wording in our bylaws very carefully, and that has been very helpful at times.

"A man was presented for membership some time ago. His name was Ron Caliburn."

"I seriously doubt that," said Bentley.

"Rightly so," said Miguel. "You will also doubt his statement that while his mother's family had Swiss roots, his father's people were Welsh."

"With some Scots blood, right?"

"Am I missing a joke here?" asked Yorga.

"Yes," said Miguel. "Ron and Caliburn are the names of King Arthur's weapons, his spear and his sword. According to the Welsh-Scottish annals, the only true historical record to even mention Arthur, he used those two weapons to kill 960 Saxons at the battle of Badon Hill. Personally, you understand; not by delegation."

"That's a lot of Saxons," said Yorga.

"The record states that he stood for three days and three nights, bearing on his shoulders the cross of Christ, and was victorious," said Bentley.

"Metaphorically, about the cross," clarified Miguel. "It was on his tunic; an emblem."

"So that's 960 Saxons in 72 hours. Busy man." Yorga sipped his coffee and waited for the point.

"Works out to a Saxon every four minutes," said Bentley. "Presumably he got a few Saxons ahead, had a bite to eat, got a few Saxons ahead, took a nap, you know, that sort of thing."

"To be sure, it was the later version of the annals – the revised entry – which recorded that feat. Still, the names Ron and Caliburn, in such a context, are very highly suspect," said Miguel.

"I always thought King Arthur's sword was named Excalibur," said Yorga, sipping his coffee.

"That's from Sir Thomas Malory, writing in his *Le Mort D'Arthur*, in the twelfth century," said Miguel. "Nearly a thousand years after King Arthur himself."

"If he even existed," said Bentley.

"Someone fought for the Britons on Badon Hill, using old Roman tactics," countered Miguel. "So the evidence…" He shrugged.

"Okay, so this guy, Rob Excalibrun…" said Yorga.

"Ron Caliburn," said Miguel. "Obviously, I doubted his story right away. Now, as I said, we wish to freely regulate our own membership. Gun rights are a touchy subject in this state. We do not want to have people among us who will discredit the rest of us; we who simply enjoy a bit of sport from time to time."

"What was wrong with Caliburn, aside from the suspect name?"

"He seemed to have a very unhealthy interest in knowing where members obtained their firearms, and how. In discussing the matter with him, it seems that he dealt in firearms himself. In particular, he was interested in guns of uncertain provenance."

"Uncertain provenance." Yorga's eyes narrowed. "Is that a nice way of saying that the guns were stolen?"

"Well, the category might be wider than that. But I took away from our conversation the very strong impression that he was in the habit of selling guns he did not actually own, or perhaps that did not officially exist."

"Like Herb's guns that were supposedly officially destroyed, but weren't quite."

"Yes. Something like that, perhaps. To be honest, I am not certain if he was in the business of distribution, or of collection."

"You think he was buying stolen guns?"

"I think that if we had accepted his membership, a large number of our guns would have been reported stolen within the next few months, and then we would have had a hard time finding Mr. Caliburn."

Bentley broke in. "Can anyone describe him? Could we have a sketch artist give us a face to work with?"

"It was a while ago, and I am not good with faces. But we are fortunate to have state-of-the-art security cameras in our club buildings." He slid a paper across the table. It had two photos printed on it: one showing a man's face, and the other the same man's head and shoulders, at a slightly oblique angle.

Bentley glanced at it and slid it to Yorga.

"Might be slightly familiar, but I'm not sure," said Yorga. He passed the photo across to his partner.

"That's no one I recognize," said Bentley. "How did he take it when you rejected his application?"

"Not well. We told him that we would let him know, and then we sent him a letter telling him that we regretted to inform him of the membership committee's decision, and that sort of thing.

"Two weeks later, we had an attempted break-in. Nothing was stolen, just some damage to a gate and to one door. From the camera footage, we were able to see that Mr. Caliburn was one of the raiders."

"After your guns, you think?"

"Fortunately, our storage lockers are in an inside room, with excellent security, as you saw when you came to visit. With that other fellow... I don't recall his name, off the top of my head."

"Detective Yoshi Kojiro," said Bentley. "And please allow me to apologize for his rudeness."

"Think nothing of it. We understand that one may not always select one's workmates." Miguel drew a breath. "As it happened, they were not even able to break into the kitchen. We have a good security system."

"Or they were bad at breaking in," said Yorga. "So, who sponsored him?"

"After the break-in, we had words with the member, who confessed that he had met Caliburn at a party, and Caliburn had offered him three thousand dollars for the sponsorship. The member agreed to the scheme, but said that he never received the money he had been promised."

"Not surprising," said Yorga.

"We did ask the member to resign his membership, and he had been one of our less-active members, anyway. I heard that he sold his farm and moved over to the other valley, to be with some of his family there."

"What was his name?"

"Carl Bechstein. I doubt that he was involved, aside from selling his name."

"We should check it out anyway," said Yorga.

"As you choose, Detective. Now, I must not know any details, but I assume that you have taken some steps to deal with the very serious charges that are facing both you, Franz, and also Herb?"

"Steps have been taken," said Bentley, "Like a stolen stairway at a dance recital."

"Ah, I see. Well, Gentlemen, it has been a pleasure to speak with you thus," said Miguel, finishing his coffee and putting down the cup. "But I have places to be, and it would be good for me not to be seen here."

The men rose and shook hands, as Miguel showed himself out. Bentley closed the door behind him, watching through the window until Tomas was behind the steering wheel.

The pickup started, and the detectives watched its taillights bounce slowly down the long dirt road until it topped a small rise and disappeared.

"Have time for a few hands of cribbage?" asked Yorga, producing a deck.

"Alright," said Bentley. "But you should know, they call me The House."

"Why's that?"

"Because I always win."

Chapter Eleven

LIEUTENANT JONES THUMBED through the manila file folders on his desk. When he was satisfied that he had addressed each issue, he opened his desk drawer and removed a 6H pencil. With the eraser, he removed a tiny, almost imperceptible, mark from his desktop.

The folders went in a very precise stack near the left edge of the desk. A ruler confirmed that the top and bottom corners of the stack were precisely one centimeter from the edge. With the pencil, Jones made a tiny dot, just at the lower right corner of the stack.

A single hair, plucked from the back of his head, where he could still afford to give one away, was then placed on top of the top folder, at a precise forty-five degree angle from that corner.

With his cell phone, he took a photograph of his desk. He stepped to the end of the desk, then took another, just to be certain.

Then, after one last glance through the windows into the squad room, to be absolutely certain that he was not being watched, he walked out the door of his office, flipping the light switch as he closed and locked the door. He did not hear the tell-tale click from the bookcase behind his desk, where a hidden camera had just shifted from day mode to night mode, but he was aware that it had happened. He resisted the urge to glance back and to make sure that the faint red glow of the infrared LEDs wouldn't give the camera away to an intruder.

Jones walked out of the old police station building. Next year, if he was still with the Salinas Police, maybe he'd be in the new police services building, planned for the old MST lot on East Alisal Street. There, he hoped, the security would be much tighter, and it might not be necessary to do so much cloak-and-dagger just to know who was reading his mail. But in the meantime...

He put the thought out of his head and jaywalked over to the old armory, then turned down Howard Street. Where it tee-intersected with Salinas Street, he jaywalked again, quickening his pace to get across the three lanes.

Then he turned against traffic, towards Gabilan Street. As he came even with the old firehouse, he watched for cars that might be hurrying up Lincoln to make the turn at Gabilan and get behind him, but he didn't notice anything unusual. He turned the corner at the old bus station.

As he approached the alley, mid-block, he rotated counter-clockwise, to catch any cars coming along behind him. Again, no cars caught his eye, so he ended the turn by stepping into the alley. He changed his pace to a jog and let himself into the back door of the Japanese restaurant. In the hallway, he paused, turning around and looking behind him. After a moment, he continued into the restaurant.

He dodged a young woman with a tray of miso soup bowls. The sushi chef glanced up at him for a millisecond before returning to the roll he was making. A waiter, recognizing a frequent customer, smiled at him as he moved past. And then he was out the front door.

A right turn, against the flow of cars. There was a plan to re-design Main Street for two-way traffic, maybe sometime in 2021, so for the next couple of years, he could keep doing things like this. After that, he'd need a new way to screen a tail.

Another jaywalk through a gap in the cars, and he was in front of the Fox theatre. He made a turn to read the poster in the coming-soon window, and a quick scan for anyone else jaywalking, or maybe just behaving oddly – but no one seemed to take any interest in him.

He slipped down the small breezeway that styled itself Midtown Lane, doing one last rotation before letting himself into the tiny diner. As he did, the proprietor locked the door behind him and turned the sign to "Closed."

A man was already sitting at a table, reading a newspaper. Jones sat opposite him, and the café owner filled a coffee cup for him, then went back to his closing routine.

"We're fairly sure it's a house at Lincoln Street and Main," said the man, lowering the newspaper and folding it. "But there are four houses there, and we're not sure which one."

Jones started to protest that Lincoln didn't cross Main, before realizing that they weren't talking about Salinas. "Are we likely to be ready any time soon?" he asked, putting sugar and creamer into his coffee. "I've got two good men tied up on this thing, and I'd like to get back to normal soon."

"Don't hold your breath," said the man. "We've got a lot of loose ends, still. And we're going to need to raid the farm again soon."

"What happened with the Mallory woman?"

"It looks like they stepped on their shoelaces," said the man, with a smile. "Couldn't even find the coke they planted. It really makes you wonder about people who lose, even when they cheat."

"Don't underestimate them," said Jones. "This is a very big deal. You remember what happened at the hotel, right? The agent they sent to clean it up?"

"That's what got this started. Without the papers that your contact sent down, we'd never have believed that any of this was going on. Not on this kind of scale."

"So where do we go from here?"

"Just keep doing what you're doing," said the man. "They'll end up tripping themselves again, just like they did in Washington."

The man smiled. Until then, his face had been so precisely mediocre that Jones wasn't sure he'd be able to describe him later. Well-shaved, no mustache, and no one single feature that was memorable. Even his clothes seemed chosen to make him blend in.

"I can only hope so, Agent Reed," said Jones. "I have no idea how to give our DA any real case."

"By the time we wrap it up, the fish will have already cleaned and fried themselves," said Reed. "The Denver office will send out a federal prosecutor, and it'll all be on them from there. We just need to keep collecting evidence. Build the case, one brick at a time."

"And of course, once the smoke clears, Yorga and Bentley will be cleared of any wrongdoing?"

"Well, as far as possible. We won't prosecute for obstruction, or anything of that sort. After all, Yorga bird-dogged this issue, and you persuaded us to open an investigation. But he was up at that hotel before you were, and he didn't find this little plot – or didn't report it if he did. And they found cocaine at Yorga's apartment."

"Seriously? You don't think that there's reason to believe it was planted?"

"Optics," said Reed. "We'll at least need to get it in front of a jury, so it doesn't look like we're revealing one conspiracy to cover up another. Also, if you get word that Bentley's about to be raided, it would be worthwhile to have someone sweep his place, like someone did for the Mallory woman."

"You'd burn Bentley and Yorga?"

"We need to get the organization behind this. We need the big cheese. There might be some collateral damage along the way."

"Over my bloody shield," said Jones, standing up. He marched out. Reed looked at the door, then at the proprietor, and found himself in a staring contest. He shrugged and headed for the door.

"So I need a security system," said Jenn, to the man across the glass counter. "Somebody in my building, they had a break-in."

"Anything stolen?" asked the clerk, a short man in a white short-sleeved shirt with a pocket-protector.

"No, but some weirdo moved a bunch of my stuff around. Put mothballs in the blankets, that sort of thing."

"Some kind of pest-control bandit, huh?"

"Yeah, so what you got to keep people out?"

"Keep 'em out, or tell you when they break in?"

"Both. I wanna catch 'em in the act."

"So, we've got locks to slow 'em down, alarms to report 'em, and cameras to tell you who they were and what they did." He took a deep breath, and nodded, rubbing his chin. "Three-tier approach, that's what you want. Slow 'em down, chase 'em off, and keep 'em running once they go."

"Whazzis gonna cost me?"

"Depends on a few things. Lemme get some parts from the back, for kind of a show and tell."

"Sure, knock yourself out." She turned her attention to a set of nanny cams in the display case.

A voice spoke from behind her. "What you are needing, Jenn Mallory, is not a security system."

She froze in her tracks. "Who –"

"Do not turn around. Who I am is not going to be the most important thing," he said, with a trace of an Indian accent. "What is most important right now is that you are not speaking to anyone who is of the police. The things in your warehouse are being removed. You are not knowing anything about them."

"You're with Louis."

"You are not saying any names," he stressed. "You are simply forgetting that you were ever involved in such a thing. If you are doing this, then the police are still not finding cocaine between your blankets, instead of the mothballs."

"You know about that?"

"Consider what I am saying as being like a warning. Now I am going, and you are not looking back at me. You are staying where you are, for five minutes, before you turn and look. And then you are not involved in anything after that, and you are not saying anything. I am speaking clearly enough, yes?"

"Yes." She nodded her assent as well.

"Goodbye."

She stood stock still, listening for a door opening and closing, or for retreating footsteps. Five minutes; three hundred seconds. She started counting down in her mind.

"Got just the thing for you," said the clerk, returning through the door from the back. He plunked down a series of boxes. "Here's your standard model stealthcam 97 ... hey, are you alright?"

"Yeah, I dunno," she said. "I'm feeling a little faint."

"Can I get you a glass of water?"

"Sure yeah, that'd be good," she said, leaning on the glass counter for support.

"Be right back," he said, disappearing again.

Kim King knocked on Bentley's door. There was a pause, and then the sound of papers rustling inside the apartment. The door locks made a snicking sound, and then the door opened just enough for Bentley to peek out.

"Just me: King," he said. "What, you thought maybe I was the pizza guy? You afraid of deliveries now? So, you gonna lemme in, or what?"

Bentley pushed the door closed, disengaged the chain, and pulled it wide open. As King walked in, Bentley discreetly tucked his off-duty pistol into the back of his pants, and lowered his shirt over it. King still noticed it.

"Hey, you really are afraid of deliveries. What's that all about?"

"So, what brings you by?"

"Can't stay. Just wanted to drop these by. Hey, you know, they use things like this in Japan, the transit people do, to keep teenagers from hanging around on train platforms. Doesn't bother us old people because we lost all of those frequencies already. But these wouldn't even work for the teenagers."

"Yeah, don't worry about that. Thanks for doing it. What do I owe you?"

"Nah, I still owe you from that thing two years ago. Forget it. Hey, gotta run. Martina's meeting me at the blue boar, by Sherwood."

"Have the beef barley soup. It's really good."

King didn't answer. He just slipped out the door and closed it behind him.

Yoshi Kojiro unlocked the door of his apartment on Pine Street. He froze as soon as he stepped inside. Something was wrong. There was a scent, like saffron, and another scent, like tobacco. A dark figure was sitting in a chair. He reached for his gun.

A hand, from behind him, caught his hand and held the gun in its holster. An arm snaked around his throat.

"Don't do anything foolish, Yoshi," said a voice in his ear. He recognized it as Louis Xeng. "We've just come to follow up on a few things. Such as what happened with the cocaine."

Louis relaxed the grip on his arm and closed the door behind them. Yoshi flicked on the lights, revealing Sandip across the room, in an easy chair.

"Don't worry," said Lou, coming around beside Yoshi and gesturing into the room. "We're just here to talk. If it were the other kind of visit, there would be plastic on the floor, and you wouldn't have seen us."

Yoshi walked in and sat down, cautiously, nervously. Sandip smiled. It just made Yoshi more uneasy. Sandip had that kind of smile. To Sandip's credit, he didn't actually intend to make Yoshi uncomfortable. He merely had a highly skewed perspective on the facial expressions that he presented to others.

"So," said Louis, taking a seat on the couch, opposite Yoshi, and at a right angle to the chair in which Sandip sat. "Tell me about the re-appearance of the cocaine. Our man insists that he hid it between the woman's blankets."

"I come in, right, like I always do. We send the dog, he gets nothing. I do the search anyway. Nothing. Makes me look stupid as hell. It's not my fault that raid went bad, by the way. Don't blame that on me. I did my part."

"Nobody is blaming, nobody is shaming," said Sandip. He crossed his legs at the knees.

"So I come in to the office the next day, and my desk looks totally normal. I open the third drawer on the left, and there's the cocaine."

"Just like that?" asked Louis.

"Just like that. The very same bag, same tape on the outside, everything."

"And how are you remembering exactly the way of the tape on the bag?" asked Sandip.

Yoshi shook his head. "It's all the same bag. How much cocaine do you think we have? You think the stuff grows on trees?"

"Wait," asked Louis. "It's the same bag?"

"Yeah, it's a kilo from a bust down on Pajaro Street, back in 2008. It's been sitting in the evidence room forever. Case got delayed, one defendant got a plea-bargain, the prosecutor moved out of the county, yada yada. So we borrowed it. Might as well do some good and not just take up space."

"When was the last inventory?"

"Inventory? Ha. We did one, maybe six years ago, when I first got here. But it was just like, here's the list of stuff, we still got all this? Yes. Here's the cases coming up next month, we got this? Yes. Okay, forget the rest, back to your normal jobs."

"So no one will miss this kilo?"

"Just like nobody is missing these guns. The really ugly ones, low value, we send 'em to get destroyed, so that we have an explanation for what happened to the rest."

Louis leaned back and stared at the ceiling for a moment.

"What will you be doing when the cases come to trial?" asked Sandip. "Won't you have to produce the cocaine for each one of the trials?"

"Yeah, so we put the kilo into the right evidence bag, and there it is, your honor, the bag we found at the Mallory place. Or the Fallguy place."

"Pfalzmann."

"Whatever. Or the Yorga place."

"And then what are you doing for the next trial?"

"You know these guys are going to plead out, right? What else can they do?"

"Humor Sandip," interjected Louis. "What if they don't, and you've already used the cocaine at the first trial? Suppose that there is not a fresh bag turning up in the drawer of your desk each time."

"We just take the first kilo, cut off the bag, and put it in the second bag. Boom, new evidence in a new case. Just like that."

"And some wiseguy of a lawyer proves it's already been in some other trial? Or better yet, there's two trials going on at opposite sides of the courthouse? What are you gonna do, run up and down the hallway?"

"Worst case, I'll put some baking soda in a bag and run it down the hall to the other trial. I mean, who's gonna look that close, right?"

"A smart lawyer is going to have his own lab test all of the evidence, including any alleged cocaine." Louis shook his head.

"So we switch it after the lab tests," said Yoshi, with a bit of a whine to his voice. Why were these guys being so harsh? He was doing his part, making the arrests. It wasn't his fault if there wasn't enough cocaine.

"How are we knowing that the package that we have is even really the same cocaine?" asked Sandip. "It is out of our sight several times including the very badly failed incident with the Mallory woman."

"Come on," said Yoshi. "I'd have to be pretty stupid. Besides, it's the same tape. I've got pictures on my phone from every bust we've done."

Louis and Sandip exchanged a glance.

"So," said Louis, "You have photographic evidence on your person, right now, showing that we allegedly discovered the same parcel of cocaine at multiple crime scenes? And you're just carrying this around on your personal phone?"

"Well, when you put it that way…"

"Sandip," asked Louis, "Do you have any pictures on your phone, perhaps, from the guys up in Washington State, when the money-laundering end of this operation went badly?"

"Of course not," replied Sandip, without taking his eyes off of Yoshi. "I would not be so stupid as to be having evidence on my person of crimes that I was in the act of committing. But I can tell you that the men who were responsible for that fiasco paid very dearly."

Louis shook his head. "In particular, a picture of Oleg, and the very terrible thing that happened to him, would go nicely here. I think Yoshi might learn from him. Do we at least have some plastic sheeting in the trunk of the rental car?"

Yoshi drew in his breath and held it.

"Clearly I have overlooked it," said Sandip. His eyes still had not budged from Yoshi's. Sandip was trying to intimidate Yoshi, and it was working. Yoshi was honestly hoping that Sandip would eventually blink.

"Then I suppose that this will have to be a warning." Louis stood up and walked to the door. "Give me your cell phone."

Yoshi drew the cell phone, carefully, with slow movements, and watched as Louis ejected the SIM card and the memory card. Both of these went into Louis' pocket.

"If you are having any data up in the clouds," said Sandip, carefully, "I would be deleting it right now and erasing the entire account."

Sandip continued to stare at Yoshi. Then he drew a silenced semi-automatic pistol from his inside pocket and let it rest in his hand. His finger hovered near, but not on, the trigger.

"You would be very wise if you were not moving," he said, as he slowly rose to his feet. He circled slowly around until he was behind Yoshi, never taking his eyes off the detective. Then he backed to the door, where Louis was waiting.

In one smooth maneuver, Louis opened the door for Sandip, then followed him through, allowing it to close behind them with a loud click.

Yoshi finally let out his breath.

Chapter Twelve

YOSHI WAS AT his desk when Bentley arrived, which was a first. More intriguing still, Yoshi's eyes were not glued to an electronic device. Instead, he was staring intently at a report of some kind. He looked up as Bentley approached.

"About time you got here," he said. "We've got a clue in the case."

"Another ATM sighting?"

"Nope. Close to home this time." He spun the report and slid it across his desk, onto Bentley's.

"Let's say I haven't had enough coffee yet to make sense out of that," said Bentley. "Give me the two-minute rundown. The condensed version."

"Sundaram over in professional training? He does a practical for all the newbs, once a month."

"He's in training now?"

"Yeah, Taylor took over gangs."

"Never thought Sundaram would give that up."

"Can I get on with it?"

Bentley gave Yoshi a surprised look. It was rare to see him so intense. "Hey," said Bentley. "You feelin' okay? You're lookin' a little pale."

"I'm fine. But Sundaram found something."

"What was that?"

"Yorga's fingerprints."

That thought gave Bentley a quick thrill. Where were they found? If Yorga's fingerprints had turned up, say, at that apartment on Lorimer...

"Yeah," continued Yoshi. "And they're fresh. Within 60 days. Max." He tapped the paper.

"Where did they turn up?"

"See, that's it, right?" Yoshi grinned. "Sundaram, when he does the practical, like every eight weeks or so, it's fingerprints. So he has the probies and the explorers dust the keybox in the City Hall garage. Lots of nice prints, they lift 'em, run 'em through NCIC, and they see how to trace the evidence, who was there, in what order, what cars they took, all that."

"You can do that? Legally, I mean, because with privacy, city employees, you know?"

"Sundaram says if they don't want their prints run, they shouldn't leave 'em laying around. Anyway, guess whose prints came up this time?"

"Yorga."

"Yup. Looks like maybe about two weeks ago or so, he went through and opened every single car in the pool."

"Why would he do that?"

"Well, that's the question. But it means he's here."

"Here?" Bentley couldn't resist turning in a circle, scanning the squad room as if he thought Yorga would be sitting at a desk.

"Not here," snapped Yoshi. "In Salinas! He's hiding right here under our noses."

Bentley stroked his mustache. "Scary thought."

"We didn't pick him up on the cameras, though," said Yoshi, with a slight sigh. "Woulda been nice to see where he came from."

"You know," said Bentley, "If it was me, and I wanted to get into the garage, I'd come in the door on Church Street, into the permits department, and then take the elevator down. I don't think there's any cameras over there, but you could ask somebody in permits if they saw him go through."

"Think they'd remember from two weeks ago?"

"Yorga's a big guy. He's kinda hard to miss."

"What are you gonna do?"

"I got maybe something from an informant, just a name, hardly even that. Probably nothin' but I need to follow it up or it'll haunt me."

"Right," said Yoshi. "Back in a flash."

When Kojiro was out the door, Bentley casually sat down at his computer and ran an NCIC search on Ron Caliburn. It came back empty, offering instead a set of offenders named Claiburne or Calibso. He ran it again, as an alias this time. Two hits.

The first was a report from 2015, involving a check-kiting scheme out of the Shasta County. No connection to guns or drugs, no active leads, no one actively running the case. A cold trail at best.

The second was from Kelso, Washington, and involved a smuggling ring. It sounded promising. Bentley copied and pasted the summary into an email, and addressed it to himself. Something to follow up.

Tomas Miguel walked into the Alisal Street Grill. He paused for a second after entering. There were two steps down from the door to the main dining room, and the contrast with the bright sunlight outside rendered him slightly blind for a moment.

A man in a light brown suit raised a hand, waving Tomas over to his table. Miguel, as his eyes adjusted, carefully navigated the steps and made his way across to the table.

"Thank you for seeing me," Miguel said, as he slid into a padded seat.

"My pleasure," said the other man. As he spoke, a waiter appeared at Miguel's elbow.

"The beef goulash special, and whatever is on tap," said Miguel, waving away the proffered menu. The waiter nodded, bowed slightly, and vanished.

"I should have tried the goulash, but I went with the spaetzli at the last second. This Bolognese sauce…"

"The entire menu is outstanding," replied Miguel. "But, if you have not tried the goulash – Well, Harold, I am happy for you that one day you will have that experience. Enjoy the anticipation."

"I'm fairly sure, Tomas, that you didn't ask me here to talk about culinary matters," said Harold, sipping from a wineglass.

"Not at all," said Miguel. "I wished you to know that I am going to be seeking an evidentiary hearing in the matter of Herbert Pfalzmann."

The waiter appeared with Harold's spaetzli, smoothly sliding it in front of him without breaking the flow of the conversation.

"You've picked a tough one," said Harold, as he spread his napkin in his lap and tossed his tie over his shoulder. "The evidence is pretty solid."

"Was the cocaine tested in the field?"

Harold picked up his fork. The aroma of the Bolognese sauce wafted to his nose, making him flare his nostrils. It would be rude to start before Tomas, but the scent was so wonderful that he was tempted anyway.

"Field tested, and then we scheduled the lab test. The lab is way behind, you understand."

"Yes, and that is another concern. My client is entitled to a speedy trial, after all."

"Of course, but you have to be reasonable."

"But an innocent man is sitting in the county jail," said Tomas. "Perhaps for no reason."

"Oh, they're all innocent, until the plea agreement," said Harold. The waiter appeared a second time, and a plate of beef goulash materialized in front of Tomas. "Come on, it was a full kilo, and we believe it was nearly pure. Two and a quarter pounds, Tomas."

"I have reason to believe that the cocaine – well, that it isn't actually cocaine."

"I suppose that Pfalzmann wraps up his powdered sugar in layers of plastic and electrical tape to keep the ants out of it."

"It is not criminal to be strange," said Tomas, raising a morsel of beef on his fork.

"You'll pardon me if I wait for the lab report."

"I would be satisfied with a field test, so long as it is done in the hearing, before the judge."

"We also found guns."

"I'm sure you did," said Tomas. "We'll get to those in turn. For now, I'm much more concerned with the alleged cocaine. It seems to be the single biggest factor in the complaint."

"Alright, I'll bring an officer and meet you *in camera*," said Harold. "I'll have one of our best people do the field test right in front of you."

"No need," said Tomas. "I'll bring my own."

"Suit yourself," said Harold. He was alarmed, deep down, by how complacent and cooperative he felt, but there was something about the pleasant ambiance of the restaurant – or perhaps about the incredible Bolognese – that simply made it unimaginable to be combative.

Had Tomas brought this to him in his office, he would never agree to a hearing at the drop of a hat. But Harold felt an odd sense of wellbeing, as if there could be nothing wrong in the world so long as this place, and this sauce, existed. It was like a small slice of heaven, disguised as a bar and grill.

"Speaking of the guns," asked Tomas, casually, "Have they been test-fired?"

"No," said Harold. "The evidence technician found one of them – well, the rifle, the barrel was bent, and the pistol, the cylinder wouldn't line up. Bad timing. Unsafe, both of them."

"What a shame," said Tomas. "Of course, that will make it hard to prove that they're really the guns that were allegedly destroyed."

"It's illegal to possess guns with filed off serial numbers. So we'd have him on gun possession charges, even if you're right about the cocaine."

"Good point," said Tomas, pushing away his plate and leaning back in his chair. "Though nothing is truly certain until trial. I don't suppose you'd be interested in a small wager, would you?"

"Do you know something I don't?" asked Harold, sipping from a small glass of red wine.

"In the matter at hand, of course I always comply with rules of discovery," said Tomas. "This is not a game. Justice is never a game. A man's freedom is at stake."

"It always concerns me," said Harold, "When someone makes so strong a protestation of innocence. Wasn't there something in Hamlet about that?"

"I would have to ask a scholar," said Tomas, wiping his lips with a napkin. "Please, the meal is on me."

"Red flag," shouted Chuck. "Someone just ran an NCIC check on Ron Caliburn."

Louis, who had been casually reading the newspaper, lowered it and looked at Chuck. "Who?" he asked.

"Gimme a minute," said Chuck. "It came from Salinas Police, but I can't tell which terminal."

"If it's Yoshi doing it, He is endangering the whole operation. Perhaps he is being terminal," said Sandip.

"Looks like – it's Bentley. Ran two searches, a name search and an alias search. He's definitely on the trail."

"Not for long," said Louis. "It's time to burn him. Where did he hear that name?"

"Want me to call Yoshi and have him go set up Bentley for a raid?"

"No, better for us, if Yoshi is surprised," said Louis. "Sandip and I will do it. Where is the cocaine?"

"In the trunk," said Sandip. "I am waiting for you to decide where we are going to be next."

"Now you know," said Louis.

Bentley's phone rang. The caller ID didn't show a name. It was just an address. His address.

"Excuse me," said Bentley. "I've got to take this. CI." He walked out the back door, where the cars were parked, on the lot at Howard and Church. He looked around, at the courthouse, the post office, and the back of city hall. In all, things seemed fairly quiet.

The call was from his alarm, telling him that someone was at his apartment. And since he lived alone, that didn't bode well. He swiped his finger on the phone a few times, and he soon had a view from the security camera in his living room.

Someone was there, stealthily placing something under his couch cushions. Broken guns, no doubt, with filed-off serial numbers. And the white package, wrapped in plastic, that the South Asian man was hiding in the credenza – it looked oddly familiar, to say the least.

Yorga couldn't sweep the apartment for him, like he had done for Jenn Mallory: Yorga was in Chualar. There was really no one else to trust with it. He'd have to do it himself, if he could get away.

There was usually a break of almost six hours, Yorga had said, between the plant and the search. Time for the drug planters to get the raid organized, and the suspect into custody. A few minutes from now, Yoshi would be getting a call, to tell him to keep Bentley busy while they got the warrant.

If Bentley was in the door as soon as the planters were out of sight, he could make it work. Maybe. As long as they kept the timing on track.

Chapter Thirteen

JUDGE SALAZAR SMILED as he opened his chamber door. "Please, Gentlemen, step inside." Tomas seated himself comfortably in front of the judge's desk. Harold hovered for a moment, then took the seat beside him. The third man, in a tan uniform with a shiny bronze badge, stood in the corner, behind Tomas.

"I understand," began Judge Salazar, "that we can perhaps expedite one of the cases in the docket, by this quick hearing?"

"I apologize for the short notice, Your Honor," said Tomas. "My esteemed colleague and I were having lunch together–"

"Where?"

"The Alisal Street Grill. It's not exactly new…"

"A spin-off from *Dulce et Decorum*, right? Tomas, how do you find all the best places?"

"I am led by my stomach," said Tomas.

"Harold, what did you have?"

"The spaetzli, your honor."

"You skipped the goulash?"

"I appear to have missed a treat."

"Indeed, Though the lamb, or better still, try the jaegersnitzel… But enough food talk, it's making me hungry." said Judge Salazar. "Now, for which matter are we meeting today?"

"State versus Pfalzmann," said Tomas. "There is a question concerning a key bit of evidence, and we were thinking that if perhaps that were resolved, we might issue a writ of *habeas* –"

"We said nothing about *habeas corpus*," said Harold.

"Well, but if the man is innocent," said Tomas.

"He's not innocent," said Harold.

"We shall see. Have you the evidence?"

"It's being brought over from the lockup, right now."

"It's at the station, just across the street?"

"Yes," said Harold. "Should be here any moment."

"Excellent. I've asked Officer Dunbar, of the County Sheriff's Department, to conduct a field test – you did bring the kit?"

Officer Dunbar nodded and produced a small plastic bag containing phials, reagents, and other paraphernalia. There was a knock at the door. Harold smiled.

"That will be them." He got up and opened the door, leaning into the hallway. There were some muffled word, calm, but growing intense as they progressed. After a moment, Harold closed the door and stared at Tomas with glowing eyes.

"I don't know how you knew," said Harold, "But I'm going to find out."

"How I knew what?" asked Tomas, innocently.

"The, ah, bag of cocaine—"

"Alleged cocaine," interjected Tomas. "And there should have been two: One in the kitchen and one in the trunk of the old car."

"It has gone missing. It's not in the lockup."

"The cocaine is ... missing?" asked Judge Salazar. "Both bags? All of it? It just went missing?"

Harold nodded.

"I'll order that the indictment be amended," said Judge Salazar, "Since it would now be impossible to present a *prima facie* case on the possession charges. Any objections to that?"

Tomas shook his head: He knew better than to speak in a legal matter when it was going his way. Harold made several faces, which seemed to express disbelief, anger, confusion, and finally, a hesitant acceptance.

"We might find it, still," he said.

"The chain of custody would be very much in question, Your Honor," remarked Tomas, holding his hands as if to suggest that this was a regrettable thing. Harold covered his mouth with his hand, possibly to keep bad words from leaping out.

"No objection," he murmured.

"My apologies," said Tomas, to Officer Dunbar. "It appears that we shall not need your services after all."

The officer shrugged. He was salaried, and his pay was the same standing in the judge's chambers or out chasing felons. He nodded to the assembled barristers, and let himself out.

"It might be a bit premature to ask for a summary dismissal," said Tomas, tentatively.

"For now it would be," said Judge Salazar. "But if I were you, Harold, I'd make sure you know exactly where those guns are."

Yoshi's phone rang, and it was the ring reserved for Louis and for Louis' associates. He looked around the squad room, and then let himself out into the police parking lot before answering the cell phone call.

"One minute," he said, jogging across Church Street to the open space behind the new courthouse, by the Government Center. When he was confident that no one could hear him, he spoke again.

"Go for Yoshi," he said.

"Where's Bentley?" asked Chuck, without preamble.

"Not with me. Went to go do a personal errand."

"Get eyes on him now, and keep him in sight. We need him to be available."

"Is it going down?"

"Just make sure you know where he is, and keep him busy. That's all I know… Wait, huh? Hey, Sandip's got something."

"No, I don't …"

The next voice was very angry. "Listen to me, Yoshi, you little worm of a man, we have a very big problem right now. Why were you not informing us at once that Judge Salazar is holding an evidence hearing?"

"What? This is the first I've heard of it."

"Of course there is no cocaine, because we are busy hiding it in Bentley's apartment, and you of course have only the one bag. What is wrong with you? Get over to the evidence room and make sure that the guns are there, for that Herb Pfalzmann case, or else Louis and I will have to come see you again.

"And this time, we will bring plastic." The phone line went dead.

For the first time in his life, Yoshi considered visiting Osaka. Despite his name and heritage, culturally he was about as Japanese as a yarmulke, and he didn't speak enough of the language to get him from an airport to a decent hotel. Still, a sudden vacation seemed like a good alternative to being found on a sheet of plastic.

Yoshi wasn't at the station when Bentley got there. He stuck his head into Lt. Jones' office.

"Excuse me, Ell-tee," he said. "You seen Kojiro?"

"I don't have the Kojiro watch," said Jones, without looking up from the papers he was comparing. "You lost another partner?"

"No need for an APB and a task force this time," said Bentley. "Just curious."

"I think something came in earlier. I heard something about a warrant. You might want to get up to speed on that promptly."

He looked up at Bentley, who got the message and closed Jones' door.

Aron Salazar stopped his pickup between two green fields of arugula. He watched with dismay as a line of SUVs picked their way down the dirt road. Far off to the right, a police cruiser was threading its way down another farm road, and two more were coming in across the fields from the east, all of them converging on Herb's farmhouse.

Aron was far enough away that the dragnet closed without surrounding him. He watched silently from his pickup as the police vehicles encircled the outbuildings. He made a face, hoping that they wouldn't get stuck and need to be pulled out. Tow trucks could do a lot of damage to a field.

Officers swarmed from the SUVs, rushing to find vantage points for the raid. They collected behind sheds, then made pointing motions with their arms, dispersing to create overlapping fields of fire and continuous 360-degree coverage.

Aron carefully looked around, making sure that there was no one behind him. He felt a strong aversion to police, and this raid was not making him any more comfortable. He was far away, at least half a mile. There was plenty of room to discreetly thread his way out of the fields towards Airline highway.

He would make it an early day. The boss would surely understand.

As Aron bounced through the ruts, making his retreat, he thought he heard a distant gunshot. He stepped on the gas, throwing up a little more mud, and got out of there quickly.

The officers, all members of the task force, knew the drill. They had done this raid before, when they caught Pfalzmann, and it would go down the same way. The bullhorn at the front, the tear gas at the back, guns drawn, in on all sides at once.

Kojiro was in the second wave. He told himself that it was because he was too important to be at the front, and to risk being shot. In fact, the opposite was true: The leaders wanted him safely out of the way, where he couldn't do any damage.

The shouting started: demands for Yorga to give up at once; assurances of his safety, and instructions for his surrender. Yoshi grinned to himself. Yorga would not be safe, not after all the trouble he'd caused. Yoshi had instructions from Louis, that one way or another, Yorga was to go down hard and stay down.

He waited, hiding behind a tractor, as the tear gas and the smoke grenades led the way. The assault teams followed, and then men were swarming through the door.

Yoshi pushed ahead, through the smoke, forgetting the tear gas until it began to assault his eyes and nose.

He should have worn a mask, like the others. In moments, his eyes were watery and he could barely breathe. Still, he had a job to do, and he pressed in, coughing and gagging.

There, through the smoke; a huge shadowy figure was coming straight at him, moving fast. It had to be Yorga. He raised his pistol and fired, point blank.

Bentley's cell phone rang. He looked at the number, and it took him a few moments to place the name. He finally answered, moments before it rolled over to voicemail.

"Bentley."

"Hey, Bentley, this is Cooper, over on SWAT. Listen, I only got a second, but I thought you should know. Your partner got injured real bad, and they're taking him up to Memorial Hospital."

The line went dead.

The question in Bentley's mind – Aside from how badly Yorga was hurt – was how it had happened: Did they raid the farm again, or did Yorga go for another walkabout?

He'd have to go over to Memorial and see how bad it was, and he'd have to find a discreet way to confer with Yorga alone.

Worst case, Yorga might be under anesthetic and could be talking his head off. But that wasn't like Yorga. Even half-dead, Yorga would keep his trap shut. Still, a loose word – or, worse, what if the crime scene guys fingerprinted the groceries? Or the playing cards? Coffee mugs? How many places had he left his fingerprints?

For that matter, what if they found out Tomas Miguel had been there? He'd be disqualified from representing Yorga because he would be an accessory to Yorga's alleged crimes. He'd probably be disbarred, and could even serve jail time.

Bentley would need to alert Miguel immediately.

Miguel's Salinas offices were in an old Victorian house, where Gabilan Street meets Cayuga Street. His main practice seemed to be in the South County, but his address of record – no doubt to be near the courthouse – was on Cayuga.

The street side parking spaces were all full, so Yorga parked on the corner, with his car next to the fire hydrant. He was pretty sure that he wouldn't get a ticket, and even if he did, it was worth the risk.

He took the steps onto the high porch in two steps. A bell jingled as he opened the door and closed it behind himself. A woman looked up from her typing.

"Can I help you?" she asked.

"Detective Bentley to see Tomas Miguel, urgently."

"May I ask what this concerns?"

"Simply tell him who I am and what it's urgent."

"This is …"

"Unusual, irregular, yes, yes, all that stuff, but it's, um, extremely urgent. That I speak to him. Now."

Hesitantly, the woman rose and moved quickly to an adjacent door. She tapped at it and then stuck in her head. There were soft voices, and then she stepped back, as Miguel came through the door. He motioned to another room, and Bentley followed him in.

"Our friend was raided," said Bentley. "Apparently he was injured and is on his way to Memorial."

"You're sure of this?"

"I was just informed. I'm on my way to go see him. But if the farmhouse were fingerprinted…"

"Yes, I see your point. Say no more. I'll find out what has happened. We lawyers have our means of discreet inquiry. Thank you for the heads up."

He opened the door for Bentley to leave.

"Nothing to worry about," Bentley heard Miguel say to the receptionist, as the door closed behind him. "A witness in another case has had some complications, but we will—"

From Chualar Canyon Road to Memorial Hospital by ambulance, by Bentley's estimates, would take a little while – longer than the time since Cooper's phone call. If he got to Memorial before Yorga, there would be questions about how he knew.

Bentley decided on a detour to the squad room. If they were raiding the farmhouse, looking for Yorga, they must be holding off on raiding Bentley's apartment. He wasn't *persona non grata* yet, and it would be in best interest to act like he didn't know about the setup. He could make an excuse to swing by the hospital, and try to muddy the waters with Yorga, once the news officially broke.

Jenn Mallory was on a cross-country bus, passing through Lost Hills. Once the bus caught 5 south, she'd be on a high-speed run – or as fast as the bus could take her – for Kingman, Arizona.

Sandip's speech had been very persuasive. It was so persuasive that she had invented a family emergency, reported it to her boss at the city yard as a request for emergency PTO, and hopped the next bus out of Salinas.

She hadn't seen Mauri in a while, and Mauri would be so surprised to see her. They hadn't talked in forever – things had gotten a bit strained when Mauri was dating that cop. But that whole thing was done and over. It was a great time to renew an old friendship – especially with murderous gun-runners on her trail.

She hadn't told anyone about her plans, just in case. The bus would take her to Bakersfield, where she would wait overnight before buying a ticket to Kingman. That would give her a cutout; a place where she could have changed modes of transportation.

To a skip trace or a skilled operative, like Louis or Sandip, or even to the Salinas Police, if they were sufficiently motivated, the move would, at best, delay followers by a few minutes, or possibly an hour. It would not throw them completely off the scent.

But Jenn didn't know this. Like most amateurs on the run, she assumed that having options meant that her choices would be opaque. If she had choices, how could they know which she had chosen? She wouldn't realize that the chokepoints dictated her course and her choices.

Fortunately for Jenn, once she was out of Salinas, no one was interested in where she had gone.

Chapter Fourteen.

YORGA LAY ON his back, with his fingers interlaced under the pillow. This bed was softer and more comfortable than Herb's couch. The sheets had a clean, fresh scent, and a slight stiffness to them, where the sheets in Herb's closet had all been slightly musty.

His only complaint was the pillow itself. It was too soft, and didn't support his neck. Sleeping on his side was simply out of the question. Yorga preferred to sleep on his side, especially during this present emergency. It gave him a feeling of being more alert.

His stomach growled.

He opened his eyes to the daylight streaming through a window covered in French blinds. The blinds were turned the wrong way, and allowed the light to come in at a sharp downward angle. He made a mental note to turn them so that they slanted upwards, more effectively blocking the sun.

This room was much more modern, and it had a cleaner, brighter feel than the farmhouse, but that might have been an artifact of not being surrounded by dusty fields. He swung his feet to the floor, where they settled on a fuzzy plush rug.

He frowned. The whole place just seemed too dainty. Well, maybe Jenn had left some bacon and eggs.

As soon as Bentley arrived, Jones motioned him into his office. Bentley closed the door behind him. "So, I've got some bad news about your partner."

"Yorga?"

"Yorga? No, your partner, Kojiro."

"Right, Kojiro. Force of habit, you know. All those years working together. So, what happened to Kojiro?"

"Remember I mentioned a warrant? Apparently the task force got a tip that Yorga was hiding out in the Pfalzmann farmhouse. SWAT just did a raid on the place yesterday afternoon."

"Was he there?"

"As far as I know, Yorga's down in Guadalajara, sampling tequila and enjoying the surfing."

"Can't imagine him surfing. Seems like he'd be a little bit top heavy. Too easy to capsize."

"Yeah, well, anyway, Kojiro charged in without his gas mask. Got disoriented by the tear gas, slammed into a door, and his gun went off accidentally."

"You know, I've talked to him about his trigger discipline. It's hard to unlearn bad habits."

"Yeah, we'll get him some remedial training after the task force is done. Anyway, the concussion from running into the door made him fall down a few times getting out of the house."

"This is starting to sound like he may not have run into a door, exactly."

"Now that you mention it, the officer helping him out of the scene was the partner of the officer that he shot with his reckless discharge. But I seriously doubt that any SWAT officer, no matter how strongly motivated, would be so unprofessional as to attempt any form of unauthorized discipline on a fellow officer."

"How bad was the other officer hurt?"

"He took the shot in his body armor, but it cracked a rib. Maybe two."

"What about Kojiro?"

"Mild concussion, a few minor facial lacerations, and a black eye. He'll be taking a few days off."

"Is he still in the hospital?"

"They kept him overnight but let him go first thing this morning."

"I should see him and get his case notes."

"I doubt that will be necessary." Jones looked around the squad room, through the large windows of his office. "Also, I recently hired a housekeeper to make sure that my house is always clean. Just in case I have unexpected visitors on short notice."

"Are you inviting me over?"

"No. That was just small talk."

"Well, good morning to you, as well."

"Mind how you go, Bentley." He opened the door and then sat down at his desk. Bentley took the hint and left the office.

Kojiro wandered into the squad room around eleven. Jones had understated his injuries. He did only have one black eye – his left – and in addition to some small facial lacerations, he also had a remarkable purple patch down his left cheek, and some swelling at the joint of his jaw.

"Thought you were gonna be taking a few days off," said Bentley. Despite not particularly liking Kojiro, he winced at the man's obvious pain.

"Just a flesh wound," said Kojiro. He dropped a pink pasteboard box on the counter at the back of the squad room. "There's doughnuts," he mumbled.

"Anything out at the farmhouse?" asked Bentley.

"False alarm. Some CI got his facts wrong."

"What were you guys looking for?"

"Got some good intel that Yorga was hiding out in the old Pfalzmann place. Just like him to break into his partner's farm."

"Wasn't there?"

"No sign of him. Weird, too, 'cause the CI is seldom wrong. Guy that lives by Old Stage Road. Said he kept seeing Herb's old Chrysler running around. Figured somebody had to be living at Herb's place."

"I see," said Bentley. Normally, he would've made a crack about how all Chryslers look alike, but something about Kojiro's face would have made it seem petty. "Listen, I'm gonna grab some coffee. Want some?"

"Nah. Got tea." Kojiro held up a paper cup.

Yorga was right: Jenn did, in fact, have eggs and bacon in her fridge. He took advantage of this by frying up a breakfast fit for a king. He sat at her table, in the tiny kitchen of her little apartment, and ate slowly, savoring the coffee. Jenn had always had good taste in coffee.

Technically, he had not broken in. Once, long ago, he and Mauri had had permission to use Jenn's apartment, and that offer had never officially been withdrawn. He knew where the key was, and he knew the code.

He had seen Jenn as he got off the bus at the transit plaza on Central and Salinas. She hadn't seen him. For practice' sake, he tailed her to the Amtrak station, or rather, the greyhound office in its lobby. Friends of the Library were holding their quarterly sale in the shop beside the depot, so it was fairly easy to loiter until he saw that she was on her bus.

And if she were on a bus, given all the other mayhem going on, she was skipping town. Which meant that her apartment would be vacant. Which was good, because Yorga needed a base closer to the action.

On entering her apartment, the signs of a hasty departure were obvious. She had left coffee in the coffeemaker: If she were gone for more than a few days, that would be a science experiment before she got home. If her trip was planned, she'd have emptied it and rinsed it out. Maybe even wiped out the carafe.

Clothes were pulled from drawers haphazardly, as if she had grabbed all the clothes she could fit into a small bag, and left the rest. The drawers were left open, with garments dangling from their sides like Spanish moss.

She'd left the thermostat turned up. No sense heating a place when no one was there. Another sign of a speedy exit. Something or someone had spooked her.

Which meant Yorga had a safer place to stay, closer to town than Herb's farm. He hadn't really officially decided to move, but since he had nearly all his immediate possessions on him, once it got dark, the decision almost made itself.

He tried to think of anything he might need to go back and get from Herb's farm. Nothing came to mind. So Jenn's place was his new hideout.

Tomas Miguel, Esq., descended the seven steps from the blue Victorian house at the end of Cayuga Street. He thought of walking the two blocks to the courthouse, but shook his head at such madness. Cars and trucks were invented for a reason.

He climbed into his two-tone blue 1971 Ford pickup, pausing to admire its lines. It was a pleasure to own, a pleasure to drive, and sheer joy to admire. The truck came from a time when American automobiles were at their finest: True works of art. Even this utilitarian vehicle, designed for brutal and demanding work; even this was a sculpture on wheels.

He slid in behind the wheel and allowed his mind to be distracted by the moment. The truck handled like it had when it was new, and it felt wonderful to drive.

He parked it careful on Alisal Street, in front of the old courthouse. The cement faces, in bas relief along the cornices, looked down sedately as he dismounted. They had been there since 1934: La doña, the conquistador, la señorita, the sailor, the priest; each with a story to tell about the history of Monterey County.

He left them guarding the truck as he strolled up the steps and made his way through the courtyard. It was a garden now, but once he recalled that there had been a koi pond, with great huge lily pads. It didn't matter. He shook his head to clear the memories, and let himself into the first floor foyer.

On principle, he avoided the antique elevator. It was probably as safe as it had been in 1934, but he saw no need to take chances. The stairs brought him to the District Attorney's office. Harold, the ADA with whom he had lunched, was in his office, mumbling over folders full of legal documents.

Miguel tapped at the door.

"Ah, Tomas," said Harold, as if the interruption was more than welcome. "Please, come in."

"I can't stay long," said Miguel. "I am only here to deliver some motions."

"Evidence hearings – wait: the State versus Yorga? Are you representing Franz Yorga?"

"It shouldn't be a conflict," said Miguel. "His interests parallel Mr. Pfalzmann."

"Mallory, we dropped that case already, no evidence in that one. Turned out the detectives got a bit ahead of themselves." He offered one of the blue-backed papers back to Miguel.

"I would not be surprised. I do not wish to speak ill of the Salinas Police," said Miguel, "But a few of the recent goings-on have left some egg on their faces. Did you hear about the policeman who shot another officer the other day?"

"Yeah, we're still deciding what to do about that – hey, you're not representing Kojiro, too, are you? We didn't even charge him with anything."

"No, that one will have to go to someone else. I would have a conflict in that matter. So, the Yorga matter? We can review the alleged drugs, the alleged guns, and the alleged warrant?"

"The warrant was not alleged. It was a real warrant."

"Yes, of course. I meant to say, the warrant which may have been inappropriately issued and served. A dubious affidavit, let us say. Yes, that sounds nicer."

"I don't like where this is going."

"Harold, you understand, I have only the warmest regards and the highest respect for you. But I must go where Justice leads. And speaking of going, it is almost time for lunch."

"The Alisal Grill again?"

"No, the sushi place in Old Town. The one that used to be called Shogun."

"I remember that place. The Tokugawa box used to be divine."

"Yes, well, the new owners do things a bit differently, but the fried rolls are fantastic."

"We'll have to go one day."

"One day soon. Until the hearing, then."

Miguel let himself out, relieved the cement faces of their guard duties, and circled around the block, to point the truck at Old Town and his lunch.

Tina Calucci went to lunch wearing her jacket. The day was warm enough that it wasn't necessary, and she draped it over the back of the chair in the little diner off Salinas Street, across from the planning department.

It was a bit oversized for her small frame, which made it look a bit bulky on her. Usually, that would have bothered her. Today, it was something she would just have to live with.

She wore it when she left the diner. She walked halfway down the next block of Salinas street, then jaywalked near the old armory. On Howard street, she paused. Anyone paying attention to her would have seen someone step out from the back door of one of the businesses that faced Alisal Street.

If Tina were asked about it, she would simply say that she was distracted by her thoughts, and almost walked into a stranger. It took a moment to apologize, and then she was back, on her way to the Police Department offices at 200 Lincoln Street.

When she was safely back at her desk, in the police evidence locker, she removed her jacket, and put the three packages of white powder into a cardboard box on one of the shelves. Then she phoned Sandip and reported the job done.

Bentley's door opened to Sandip's picks, just as easily as it had the last time. The door did not squeak, and there was no danger of Bentley being there. Others had eyes on him elsewhere.

Sandip moved quickly. A broken pistol went under a couch cushion. It was loaded with the wrong ammunition, so that even if Bentley managed to make it useful, it still wouldn't shoot. As Louis was always saying, a wise man does not arm his enemy.

The starter pistol with the barrel obstruction drilled out – A crude homebuilt contraption – went under the mattress of the bed. The package of cocaine went into the floor vent in the same bedroom. It was a fresh package of cocaine, taped as similarly to the pictures as possible.

Yoshi could play with his one kilogram from the evidence locker, but Sandip would make sure that Yoshi's laziness did not spoil the plan.

It had been a long drive from Santa Clara, and he was feeling the effects of the coffee. He and Louis were going to stake out the building, to see if Bentley sent in a cleaner. He might not have another opportunity for a while, so he stepped into Bentley's bathroom.

As he was zipping up afterwards, he heard a clicking sound behind his left ear.

"Freeze," said Yorga, pushing open the blue plastic shower curtain and stepping out of the bathtub.

Sandip wondered if it were possible to twist away from Yorga, grab the gun from the small of his back, and shoot, before being shot himself. While he was doing the math, Yorga grabbed his gun.

Louis is not going to be liking this, Sandip thought.

Louis began to get uneasy when Sandip hadn't returned after ten minutes. The first time, it was in-and-out in under five. He supposed that Sandip might have done something foolish, like answering a call of nature, so he waited five more minutes.

Fifteen minutes after Sandip had left the car to plant the evidence, Louis got out of the car and headed into the building. The door was locked, as if Sandip had been here and gone. But in that case, why weren't they both sitting in the car, waiting to catch the sweeper?

Louis' pick-gun made fast work of the lock. He opened the door slowly, scanning for a trap. Nobody was visible in the living room, so he carefully moved to the hallway. Again, no signs of life.

His pistol led the way through the bedroom, the bathroom, and the kitchen. When he had checked everything, he made a second pass, looking for the planted evidence. It was as if Sandip hadn't even been here at all.

Had he gone to the wrong apartment? Had Sandip?

Louis let himself out of the apartment, careful to make sure that no one saw him. He checked the apartment number, and matched it against the notes. That was Bentley's apartment, and Sandip had just disappeared in it without a trace.

The sweeper. It had to be the person who had swept Jenn Mallory's apartment; and the same person that he and Sandip had intended to ambush here at Bentley's. Whoever it was, now he had Sandip.

Louis said a curse under his breath. Sandip was always doing this: getting into trouble, and making Louis pull him out. He had no discipline; none at all. The situation in the train station at San Diego; that was all Sandip's fault.

Louis was tired of it. He would talk to Caliburn, once this deal was done. This as far as Louis went.

Sirens, outside, made him pause just inside the doorway. A black-and-white police cruiser cut down the block, lights blazing, then whipped left at the corner. When the car was gone, Louis strolled casually to his car, started it, and drove after them.

His guess proved correct: Near an elementary school, the cruiser suddenly dove towards the opposite curb and stopped there, blocking the oncoming lane. The doors flew open and the police officers, guns drawn, took positions behind the open doors.

He cursed as he drove by, noticing the subject of their ardent attention. It was Sandip, standing against a chain link fence with one hand near his chin. It looked like that hand might be cuffed to the fence.

It was too late to worry about it now. In his rear view window, he saw another police car pull up behind the first, and then a police car passed him from the other direction. He idly wondered what would be the standard bail for possession of drugs and firearms, while cuffed to a schoolyard fence. More than Louis was going to shell out; that was certain.

Bentley's phone buzzed. *Snap goes the trap,* it said.
Too bad, replied Bentley. *The place is a mess.*
No, I just saw your cleaning lady leave.
Bentley deleted the conversation, and pulled the SIM card out of his phone. He dropped the SIM card into his paper-clip dispenser, and casually put the phone itself into the wastebasket.

Two suits that Bentley didn't recognize walked up behind him. Kojiro, across the desk from him, stood up and cleared his throat.

"Bentley," he said, "I'm gonna need you to put your service piece on the desk."

"Say what?" said Bentley.

"Your service piece. Really gently, pull it out and lay it on the desk blotter."

"You want me to clear all these files first?"

"Just put it on top of the files."

"Okay." He pulled the Sig Sauer out of his shoulder holster and laid it on top of a stack of file folders, next to an old cup of a liquid that was impersonating coffee.

"And your off-duty."

Bentley leaned down to remove the five-shot .38 snubnose from his ankle holster. He straightened up slowly, and carefully laid it alongside the Sig Sauer.

Then he pushed his chair back and stood up.

"Thanks for not making this ugly," said Kojiro. "Sorry it had to go like this."

"Actually, you're not," said Bentley. "But that's just how the cookie crumbles."

"Wanna put your hands behind your back?" asked one of the suits, touching Bentley's elbow.

"Not particularly. Care to tell me what this charade is all about?"

"You don't know?" asked Kojiro.

"Not a clue," said Bentley. "My conscience is clean."

"It's, um, you and the gun thing."

"You actually have to be more specific," said Bentley.

"Detective Byron Bentley," said the suit by his left elbow, "You're being charged with several counts of possession and sale of stolen property. In addition, there may later be charges of larceny, conversion, and other charges related to illegal drugs."

"See," said Bentley. "That's how you do it, Yoshi. Nice, even, clear, and professional tone of voice, using professional wording, and a professional demeanor."

"You have the right to remain silent," said the other suit, "And the right to an attorney."

At Bentley's apartment, one of the suits showed Bentley the search warrant. Bentley skimmed over the first page, and then nodded to the men.

"I'm not consenting," he said, "But I won't try to stop you. Just make sure Kojiro doesn't shoot up the place. I'm hoping to get my cleaning deposit back at the end of the lease."

"Shut up," said Kojiro.

"Oh, there he is," replied Bentley. "The Yoshi Kojiro we all know."

Kojiro's hand dropped near his holster, but one of the suits grabbed his elbow and stopped him. "Let's just get on with it," he said.

Yoshi used the Bentley's key to open the door. One of the suits stayed with Bentley, while the other helped search. There was no gun under the seat cushions. There was no gun in the bedside stand. And there was no bag of white powder to be seen.

Yoshi wasn't concerned. Maybe Sandip had gotten creative. It wouldn't be the first time he had gone off the script with his setups.

"Bring in the dog," said Yoshi.

A uniform stuck his head around the corner from the hallway. "We're trying. He won't come into the building."

"What do you mean, he won't come into the building?" asked Yoshi. "It's not an option. He's a specially trained police dog, isn't he?"

He walked out into the hallway and could see the Canine Officer, out on the sidewalk, pulling on the leash of an adamant German shepherd. The shepherd was sitting down, pushing backwards with his hind legs, and had his forelegs locked against the sidewalk. The dog whimpered, as if he were being tortured.

"He doesn't want to go any farther," said the K-9 Officer. "Never seen him like this."

"Pick him up and carry him," said Yoshi.

"That's against protocol," said the officer. "Besides, how would we know if he indicated? Tell you what, I'll walk him down to the corner, walk him back, and then we'll see."

Yoshi said a bad word and went back inside.

"You know," said Bentley, "If I knew what you were looking for, I might be able to help. What did it say on the warrant? Firearms and drugs? I think I have some aspirin in the bathroom."

"You've got a kilo of cocaine somewhere in this apartment," said Yoshi. "A certain confidential informant delivered it to you, and you payed him for it."

"Nice fairy tale." Outside, there was the sound of a car pulling away. An officer stuck his head around the doorway and nodded to Yoshi.

"We're gonna try a different K-9 unit," said the officer. "This dog's spooked for some reason."

"Hopefully a dog with a smarter handler," snapped Yoshi. He flipped over a couple of couch cushions, and yanked open Bentley's microwave oven.

"That would be a bad place for guns," said Bentley. "You're not supposed to put metal in the microwave."

Yoshi slammed the microwave shut.

There was a howl from outside, followed by a growl, some snapping sounds and a couple of bad words. Yoshi hurried outside to see what was wrong.

The second dog, a retriever, was in the back of the canine unit, growling at the handler. An officer in uniform turned to Yoshi.

"We got about three yards from the door, and the dog started howling. Wouldn't take another step. Snapped at the handler, handler let go of the leash, and now we can't get the dog out of the car." The officer shook his head. "I don't know what the deal is with this apartment, but the dogs think it's got bad voodoo."

"Bad voodoo?" Yoshi's ears turned red. "Of course it does. Every place Bentley goes has bad voodoo."

He stormed back inside, and went into Bentley's bathroom and pulled out his cell phone. It was muted. He didn't remember doing that, but, sure, maybe he had.

There was a text message from Louis. It was about 30 minutes old.

Hold off on plans, it said. *No egg in the nest.*

Wish I'd known that 30 minutes ago. Now what do I do? thought Yoshi. One of the suits walked over to the bathroom door and leaned inside.

"What do you want to do?" he asked.

"Um, yeah, wrap up the search. We'll find our informant and get better information."

"And, what about Detective Bentley?"

"Haul him back to the station and book him into the holding cell."

"Um," said the suit.

"Yeah," said the other suit, from the living room. "You said the evidence was here. We've got nothing to book him on."

"Trust me," said Yoshi.

"I'm not taking responsibility for a false arrest," said the suit in the living room. "And he's a cop. One of us, even if he is plain-clothes. I'm cutting him loose." He turned Bentley around and un-cuffed him. "Sorry for the confusion, Detective."

"No hard feelings," said Bentley. "I'd love to do the same for all of you." He reached into his pocket for his cell phone. "Which one of you jokers has my cell phone?"

The assembled officers looked sheepishly at each other and collectively shrugged.

"Yeah, never mind," said Bentley. "I'll draw a fresh one. Someone wanna give me a ride back to the station?"

Yorga's vantage point, in the small market on Central, diagonal from the school, allowed him to watch the drama unfold. As satisfying as it was, on a personal level, to watch the arrest of the man who had tried to set up Bentley's apartment, it was more interesting that a single dark gray sedan – It looked like a midsized BMW – had circled the block twice to get a view of the arrest.

He jotted down the license plate, and a quick description of the driver – East Asian, possibly Chinese; dark glasses, no facial hair, somewhat short in stature, or else slumped low in the car. This would be the first man's accomplice, looking for a way to get him out of this jam.

That might be a big task to take on. It wasn't likely that the arrestee was going to be let off with a warning. He had a suppressed 9mm pistol in his jacket pocket, not functional, but well within the definition used by the gun-free zone law.

He was not going to attack the arresting officers with it, though. The pin that engaged the slide return spring was in Yorga's pocket.

If that wasn't enough, the suspect had a drilled out starter pistol in his pants pocket, and a kilogram of cocaine in his jacket. Bail was going to be astronomical.

The storekeeper, by the window on the other side of the door, gave Yorga a look, as if to ask if he was going to buy something. Yorga flashed his badge at him. The man nodded and went back to counting his scratchers.

Through the window, despite the layers of lotto signs and flyers, Yorga noticed a sudden shadow fall on the shopkeeper. Someone was slowly approaching from the side street. Yorga shifted his weight from foot to foot, peering around the signs, and caught a glimpse of the newcomer. It was the driver of the gray BMW.

He must've decided that he could see more if he was on foot. Or maybe he had spotted Yorga in the store. A bit more peering over lost-dog signs and beer posters: No, the new guy was staring towards the arrest. He must've had the same idea Yorga had, to use the store as cover.

The store consisted of two long aisles, leading back to the beer coolers, where they joined up again. Yorga started moving slowly down the aisle on his side, keeping an eye for the Asian man. When he reached the spot where the aisles joined, he saw the Asian man step in and move near the magazine rack, where Yorga had been.

Yorga glanced discreetly up the aisle he had just traversed, but the man was standing there by the window, holding a magazine and staring outside. He didn't know Yorga was in the shop, but Yorga couldn't go out the front; he'd give himself away.

Would this guy recognize him? The guy who was being arrested would know Yorga in a heartbeat. But unless his partner had seen Yorga leave out the back of the apartments, he'd be a complete stranger, just someone who happened to be in the store.

Or were these guys deeper in it than it looked? Were these the guys who had shot at him in San Diego? He hadn't seen the faces, not clearly. He wondered if the nine-millimeter pistol that was about to be booked into evidence would match the bullets in the warehouse down on Sampson Street in San Diego.

In that case, the guy by the magazine rack might know him on sight. Probably would know him. Had probably studied photos of him. So going out the front was out of the question.

Yorga edged over to a small wooden door marked PRIVATE and let himself through. There was a storage room, with another door behind it. Yorga could hear sounds like a toddler playing in the next room back. It was likely to a residence attached to the store. Not a promising exit.

There was a double door on one side of the storage room, probably for loading supplies in by the pallet full. It didn't seem to have any kind of alarm. Yorga slipped out through the door, letting himself onto Cassidy Street.

Close call, but it was just bad luck, having the accomplice walk in like that. Still, he might be able to do himself a favor. If the driver was on foot, the BMW had to be close by; maybe on this side street.

It turned out to be on the opposite side of the block, and as Yorga had hoped, the passenger door was unlocked. It took only seconds to find the registration and get a photo with his cell phone, but in those seconds, the Asian man left the store, and started back around the corner towards the car.

He stopped at the edge of the store, to watch as the last police car pulled away from the school. He lit a cigarette to cover the pause. That gave Yorga just enough time to close the glove box, gently push the car door shut, and duck down beside the car.

As he heard the driver's car door open, Yorga duck-walked back, moving gracefully behind the '63 Impala parked behind the beemer. He slipped in back of the Impala's taillights just as the beemer's door slammed. From his crouch by the Impala's bumper, he heard, rather than saw, the gray BMW pull away from the curb.

He casually rose up, a few inches at a time, from behind the Impala, just in time to see the BMW turn left at the intersection and head towards the downtown area.

That was way too close.

"So," explained Officer Dunbar, "We have a reagent that's already in the vial. There's nothing to measure, so there's no way for us to get this wrong."

"How long have you been doing this, Officer?" asked the judge, in a friendly tone.

"About twelve years now. Before that I was mostly on traffic and sometimes corrections duties."

"Nice," said Judge Salazar. "Now, what are we expecting this to show us?"

"Well, this is the suspect powder just now seized in the second raid on the Pfalzmann farm."

"So was it overlooked the first time?"

"No, Your Honor. Someone had been staying there in between the two raids."

"We wanted to make sure that the evidence was brought in while the chain of custody was absolutely unquestionable," interjected Harold. "We would not wish to waste any of your honor's time."

"Ah. I appreciate that, Counselor."

"But this clearly doesn't belong to Mr. Pfalzmann, since he has been in custody all this time," said Tomas Miguel. "Right, Officer?"

"I wouldn't know." Dunbar flushed slightly. "So, we have two colors we could see. There's a red color if it's a training test. We do that to show officers how the kit works, without using actual cocaine, you understand.

"And there's a blue color if it likely contains illegal alkaloids, like cocaine. Then we can do more specific field tests for which alkaloid, like is it cocaine, or heroin, or whatever; and how strong, and so on. Till we're pretty sure what we're dealing with."

"So, if it turns blue, we have…" asked Salazar.

"An alkaloid."

"And if it does nothing…"

"Then it's some other kind of white powder. We'd have to have the lab tell us for sure. Of course, the lab has to back up anything we find in the field. For evidence, you know. This is just for reasonable suspicion. It's to tell us whether or not we should make an arrest."

Judge Salazar nodded and waved a hand. He already knew the law; he was merely interested in how the test worked. "And if it turns red?"

"Then someone's messing with us. That'd mean it was the calibration reagent. Baking soda."

"Please proceed."

Dunbar made a careful incision on the plastic bag. He used the tip of a small knife to withdraw a tiny amount of the powder, lift it carefully to the vial, and drop it into the clear fluid.

The color change was immediate and obvious. Dunbar swirled it to make sure that it mixed properly, but there was no denying the result of the test.

Bright red.

Chapter Fifteen

"TOMAS, I'LL ENTERTAIN that *habeas* petition now, if you have one."

"Oddly, Your Honor, I just happen to have a writ of *Habeas Corpus* right here." He passed a copy to the judge, and another to Harold.

"Harold," said the judge, as he accepted the writ, "I don't know what sort of skullduggery is going on, but I don't like it; not one little bit. You let the DA know that."

"Of course, Your Honor," said the ADA, peering at the writ, as if careful inspection would change the fact that his cocaine had just turned into baking soda.

"And you owe Mr. Pfalzmann about five pounds of baking soda. Or six, I guess," said Tomas, with a casual and friendly smile.

Harold could not suppress his sarcasm. "I'll see that restitution is made."

"Excellent," said the judge, looking up from the blue-backed paper. "Well, I'll let you both know tomorrow on the *habeas* motion. But unless some new information comes in concerning this matter…"

Harold shot Tomas a look that would have stripped the chrome off of a bumper. He closed his briefcase for dramatic effect, and with a deferential nod to the Judge, let himself out of the chambers.

"He does not seem pleased," said Judge Salazar.

"He agreed to this hearing," said Tomas, with a grin and a shrug. "But perhaps he's not feeling well."

"What do you want me to do with the bag of powder?" asked Officer Dunbar.

"Seal it, and return it to evidence," said Judge Salazar. "I may or may not decide to make a decision on the *habeas* motion tonight."

Officer Dunbar picked up the bag, along with his test kit, and let himself out. Tomas held the door for him.

"Lieutenant," said Kojiro, once he had managed to take Jones aside, "We need to release that guy right now. He's a CI."

"Which guy is that?"

"The one who just got busted because he was cuffed to the schoolyard. That's obviously a set up. And he's one of my snitches."

"Is he on the department's official registered list of our confidential informants?" asked Jones.

"Well, no," said Kojiro. "I only turned him last week. I haven't had time to do the paperwork."

"Then he's not a CI."

"But I need his evidence. It's critical for the State task force and the gunrunning investigation."

"How is he connected to that?"

"I can't talk about that, Lieutenant. You understand."

"Right, I do understand. Still not cutting him loose."

"What about his cover?"

"It'll only be strengthened by him being in the county jail. His accomplices will know he's not a snitch, if they have to get him out on bail themselves. You can still interrogate him for his intel."

As Kojiro opened his mouth to press his case, Jones' desk phone rang. Jones shushed Kojiro with one finger while he picked up the phone.

"Out of where?" asked Jones, and then, a moment later, he said, "What were those charges?"

Kojiro noticed a troubled look on Jones' face as he hung up the phone. He shook his head at Kojiro.

"No way we're making that guy a CI. We're not going to let him get anywhere near the street. He's got warrants out of Oregon, for attempted murder, kidnapping, and a few assaults. Plus the Amtrak police down in San Diego want a word with him: Carrying concealed and escape from custody. And there could also be ties to organized crime. Still waiting for more wants."

"But," said Kojiro.

"But what? He's a really nice guy once you get to know him? He takes good care of his elderly mother?" Jones pointed to the door, signifying that the interview was over. Kojiro took the hint and left.

Kojiro made his way to the evidence locker. He looked around to make sure that no one else was there before he stepped up to the small window in the metal mesh wall.

"Yo, Socks," he said.

"I told you not to call me that," hissed Calucci. "What do you want?"

"That guy that just came in, Indian guy."

"What's the case number?"

"I dunno. He just came in. Some uni booked him."

"You realize I'm stuck in this metal cage, inside this locked room, right? I don't get the luxury of seeing people get paraded down the hallway to lockup."

"Okay, um, it woulda been a bag of coke, and a gun. Maybe a couple guns."

"You realize, that's like half our cases these days."

"Except this one was right now, today."

"Yeah, okay. I know that one." She nodded to the bank of metal lockers on the back wall. "They didn't just box it all up; they put it into a locker."

"Can you get it out?"

"Yeah, with a prybar." She gave him a look. "But that's gonna leave some marks."

"Right. Kinda obvious." He rubbed his chin. "Um, look, when I was in evidence, there was this thing you could do, you kinda pull the door out a little, and you can pry the bottom corner up a little, you know, just enough to snake an arm in there. You got thin arms."

"Yeah. I'm doing that, and Jones walks in, what do I say? I dropped a quarter and it rolled into the locker? I'm doing you enough of a favor – hey, you're not wearin' a wire, are you?"

"Of course not."

"You come strolling in here, start trying to get me to talk about tampering with evidence, want me to go fishing around inside a locker? Seriously? I'm done. Get out."

"Socks! Come on."

"Don't call me that. And if I go down for helping you guys, you all go with me."

Kojiro, feeling distinctly unwelcome, left. He had a very bad feeling that Louis wouldn't like this.

He wasn't the only one with butterflies. Tina "Socks" Calucci was getting a very bad feeling about the three bags of white powder she had smuggled into the cage. Sandip was supposed to text her with the case numbers to write on the evidence bags, and then Kojiro was supposed to come in and sign the bags.

So far, the call was three hours overdue. If something happened to Sandip, and there was an audit of the lock-up, she'd have three bags too many lying around.

Her conscience began to play games with her memory. Had she possibly been careless carrying them in? Any chance she touched one of the bags with her bare hands? Or that thing they did with skin cells, trace transfer. Epithelials, all that stuff. Maybe they could even get some kind of trace off of her jacket.

She took the cardboard box down off of the shelf and carried it to the back of the cage, where the shelves would give her a moment, if anyone walked in. Then she carefully started rubbing the bags with a paper towel, to remove any fingerprints she might have left on them. If someone found too much coke on the shelves, no one was pinning it to Socks.

Bentley threaded his car around behind the old hospital, and past the outpatient center. A fork in the driveway led to a four-way intersection. Normally, he'd pull all the way up the drive to the sally port, but that was for when he was officially transferring a suspect. This was more of a private mission.

He backed up the drive that went around the side of the sally port, until he was next to the pedestrian gate. Then he turned off the engine, rolled down the window, and started to read a book.

It was about half an hour before Herb was led out the gate and turned loose. Herb looked around, not sure where he was or where to go. Bentley tapped the horn.

Herb walked quickly, in the small quick steps favored by older men when they need to move fast. He tugged the door opened and lowered himself into the passenger seat.

"I dunno if I should go nowhere with you," he said, as he buckled his seat belt.

"You're welcome to stay here," said Bentley. "But I think you ought to let me drive you home."

"I don't got a lot of choice," he said, as Bentley pulled down the drive and turned right on Constitution. "Hey, stop at the supermarket back here, I gotta get some stuff. All my food's probably gone bad while I was in."

"I took the liberty of stocking your kitchen."

Herb wasn't sure whether to be grateful, or a bit annoyed at the intrusion. "Thanks, I guess."

"Also, Yorga stayed out at your place a couple of nights. Hope that's okay."

"That dirty – I guess I could change the sheets, but what's wrong with his place?"

"Cops were looking for him there."

"My place ain't much improvement. Apparently it's like a doughnut shop or something."

"He didn't think you'd mind."

"Me and him ain't exactly on speaking terms at the moment. I was in there because of him."

"Maybe not exactly. And it may not seem like it, but he's on the side of the angels. I'm sure about that. He helped your lawyer get you out."

"Side of the angels? Yeah. Maybe. But I heard there's two kinds of angels."

"I'm sure he'll make it up to you. Was it okay in there? No trouble?"

"I kept my back to the wall and my trap shut. They all just left me alone."

"Good," said Bentley, and the rest of the drive to Chualar was quiet and uneventful.

Louis sat in his car, on Howard Street, outside the old armory. For the first time in a very long time, he wasn't sure what to do next.

If he went inside, and tried to bail out Sandip, he'd be inviting them to arrest him. If they had Sandip's fingerprints from the police cars in San Diego, they might have his as well.

And had he touched the bag of cocaine before Sandip took it into Bentley's apartment? He didn't think so, but he wasn't really certain. Caliburn was not going to like this. Honestly, Caliburn was not going to like it.

But what if Sandip's big mouth kicked in, and he started telling tales? Sandip had been part of the operation almost from the beginning, while they were still setting things into motion.

What if something he said in questioning made the police connect the money laundering operation, at that little hotel up in Washington, with the gun operation down in Chualar?

It was time to roll it all up, he decided. It was time to close all the accounts, and take all the money up to Vancouver. No one up there had the slightest clue about any of the operations. Well, maybe the RCMP was worried about illegal guns appearing on the streets, but they couldn't know where the guns were coming from.

From Vancouver, Louis could disappear into Canada without a trace. He had people in Gastown, and they could move him to Calgary, or even Winnipeg, without anyone being the wiser. Once things were closed down, he would just settle with Caliburn, and then catch a ship northbound, and vanish.

Step one of closing the accounts would be to deal with all the loose ends. Sandip could not be given an opportunity to talk. He had been useful, though often annoying. Now, however, he was nothing but a liability.

Louis did not feel even the slightest pang of regret at having to kill Sandip. Over the years, he had come to think of his colleagues as farm animals: One may befriend them, but one must keep in one's mind that someday they were going to be more useful dead.

Louis started the car. Having it near the armory was a bad idea, because it limited his options for escape. He turned right on Salinas Street and drove a block down. There was a small parking lot on the left. The lot was accessible from an alleyway north and south, or through a camera shop that faced Main Street.

It would be far enough, for now.

He locked up the car, removed a sports duffle bag from the trunk, and started jogging north, up the alleyway. He crossed Alisal Street, and found himself in a small parking lot across from the armory.

He paused to run his eyes over the big WPA-style building, and quickly spotted its Achille's heel. There was a small yard between the armory and the old firehouse. A steel ladder, terminating about ten feet off the ground, led to its roof. That would do.

When traffic permitted, he jaywalked across Salinas Street, moving with calm and deliberate steps towards the old firehouse.

Chapter Sixteen

"AFTERNOON, SOCKS," SAID Lt. Jones, with a smile. He glanced around the cage. "Everything secure?"

"Very secure, Ell-tee, as usual."

"Good, glad to hear it. You're a vital link in the chain, Socks. We couldn't do this without you." He turned on his heels, casually looking over the evidence room, like a manager doing due diligence checks.

"Thank you, Sir."

"I wasn't sure if you saw the email that went out last Thursday – oh, right, we haven't completely published that yet. Well, you probably should know, anyway."

"Sir?"

"We've had some people throwing some loose talk around, about our procedures, and we don't want anyone impugning our reputation or our integrity."

Calucci nodded, lips pursed.

"We want to be able to demonstrate that our officers have the highest integrity. If we get an accusation, we want to be able to say that it's utterly ridiculous, and that we can prove it's not true."

"I see, Sir," she said, even though she had no idea where he was going with this line of conversation.

"Don't let it out just yet, but you've heard about the new Police Services building, over on East Alisal?"

"Um, yeah, across from where the old Rodeo Bowl used to be, right?"

"There's a name I haven't heard in a while. Wow, yeah, I had forgotten all about that place. And the pizza place farther down used to be Cassidy's Pizza, right?"

"Yeah, I think it's a franchise, now."

"So we're commencing the move a little early. Like I said, don't mention it to anyone. Not even among your people on one of the other watches. We want to move the evidence room first."

"Move us, Sir?" she asked. "Won't that mess up the chain of custody reports?"

"Not if we do it right. Evidence down there is in a whole new league. You're gonna love it over there. Cameras everywhere, biometric scans to come and go, the whole deal. It's like magic."

Calucci's eyes widened, then she got control of her face and returned to normal. "I can't wait, Lieutenant."

"Anyway, starting day after tomorrow, we've got a tiger team going around the clock until it's done. Two people on here, in the cage, plus one keeping the log at the door. There'll be cameras on the door, to make sure we don't miss anything. Each box gets checked by two people here, it's sealed, logged out here, straight into the truck, officer there logs it in. Smooth as silk."

"That's – that's gonna take a lot of people, Sir."

"Yeah. And a lot of overtime. I hope you don't have any big plans for the next three weeks."

"Um, nothing big… I can shuffle things …"

"Good. For most of the team, we'll bring in some off-duty Sheriff's deputies. I can't possibly spare that many people, otherwise. I'll need you here at the cage, in case they have questions.

"You know, stray boxes, lost paperwork, things that got put away wrong stuff like that. Not that I expect any irregularities, you understand. I know that we follow the book, but, over time, weird stuff can happen, right?"

Calucci didn't want to disagree, but she also didn't want to admit anything. "We're very careful, Sir."

"I'm sure you are, Calucci. But stuff carries forward. I remember when I was a uniform. The old sergeant in charge of evidence used to keep beer on ice in the big locker back there," he said, pointing to the locker with the dodgy door.

"That was mighty bold, Sir," she said. Calucci was on pins and needles. An inventory in two days? Every box checked, sealed, and moved to a secure location? It was her worst nightmare come true.

"Yeah, but he broke off a key in the lock, so it looked like it was damaged and couldn't be used. Fact is, you can snake an arm up in, from underneath. You've got to pry it out just a little, though, and you've gotta have small arms. But that guy could get a cold one any time he wanted."

Jones smiled as if he had fond memories of the old guy with the ersatz ice cooler full of beer. "Yeah," he continued, "But later Sarge got caught trying to commit murder. Tried to drown a lieutenant, if you can believe that. He's down at Soledad, now."

He gave the counter a slap and turned as if he were about to walk away. Calucci swallowed hard. Had he just, low key, accused her of criminal conspiracy?

"Hey, ah, Ell-tee," she said, her voice rising slightly. "Um, on a different note, can I tell you something?"

"Sure, Socks, what's on your mind?"

"Um, that new detective, Kojiro? He's been hanging around here a lot. He offers to cover the cage if I need a break, that kinda thing. Little strange, you know?"

"Really?" asked Jones. "With his caseload, I wonder how he manages that."

Yorga's cell phone rang. Since it was his newest burner, and only Bentley had the number, he assumed it was Bentley.

"Yo," he said.

"Wheels are coming off," said Bentley.

"I might have loosened some of the lugnuts," said Yorga. "No go on your place?"

"Those electric buzzers? Kim King got 'em up to 130 decibels, and some ungodly pitch. Squad couldn't hear 'em but the dogs wouldn't come close."

"Hate doing that to the dogs."

"Yeah, they couldn't even get one into the building. I'll send some pig ears over to the K-9 squad, after this all blows over. To settle up."

"Those things are probably making you deaf right now. You better turn 'em off."

"Yeah, they're making me deaf for certain, but only in frequencies I can't hear. Hey, Herb's home."

"Tomas got him loose?"

"Yeah, but they can re-open with new evidence if they want. But it's not looking good for 'em."

"Nice, Herb doesn't need the grief. Hey, now you're blown, like me. You going to ground?"

"No, as far as they're concerned, I'm just under a cloud of suspicion. Nobody wants to be my friend or my enemy right now. Jones put me on admin leave."

"In that case – there's gonna be a pizza delivered to Jenn Mallory's place around six tonight. If you happened to be around there, you might get dragged into a cribbage game. Just saying."

"Delivery's not a good idea."

"Right. Okay, you pick up the pizza, and I'll pay you back when you get here."

"Might be a plan," said Bentley, as he hung up.

Watch out for this guy, texted Yorga. The next text was a car description and a license number, followed by a picture of a gray BMW and a shot of an Asian man in a convenience store.

Bentley shrugged it off and didn't reply.

Louis answered the phone on the first ring. "Xeng," he said. There was silence for a moment, then a woman's voice came on the line.

"They said never to call except in an emergency. But this is urgent."

"Yes, yes," said Louis. "Get on with it."

"In two days, they're moving evidence down to the new building on East Alisal, where the Transit yard used to be. You know?"

"Where is this from?"

"Lieutenant Jones just came in and told me. He wants me to work overtime the next three weeks to get this done."

Louis was only half listening to her. "Overtime? You are worried for overtime?"

"No, they're gonna check every box. Even the ones – you know! The boxes!"

Xeng suddenly realized the problem. "And you tell me this now?"

"Yes, I just found out."

"It is a shambles. A complete shambles." He shook his head. "I will deal with this. I will call you in one hour. Do not leave until I call you." He hung up the phone.

It was bad enough that he was going to have to deal with Sandip and in the way that he least liked: Publicly, with witnesses. He would have to escape – he had a rough plan for that, but he would have to think on his feet.

In addition, once he had gotten away, he would need to change his look and then make it all the way back to the police station, so that he could deal with the evidence. He did not trust the Calucci woman to do it.

He was learning that he could trust no one, and that if he wanted things done right … Well, there would be time to philosophize once the jobs were done.

He checked the rifle again, and made sure that it had a round in the chamber. It was an old British SMLE, stolen in Washington, recovered in Oregon, and rerouted into Louis' hands through his organization. The SMLE had once been both common and inexpensive, and very popular among hunters who were on a budget.

He had test-fired it a few times up in Santa Clara, to check the sights and to see how well it worked. It kicked horribly, but the power and the accuracy, even with iron sights, made it the ideal tool for a job such as this.

He slowly raised the extension mirror, like a periscope, to see over the parapet wall. No sign of the Sheriff's van yet.

There would be a rivalry between the city and the county, of course. He nodded slowly, to affirm this fact to himself. The only time that a county van would approach the city police offices would be for something in which full cooperation was mandatory.

Such as the transportation of prisoners to the county jail. The police did not have facilities to keep prisoner around the clock. It was far more economical to allow the sheriff's officers to do it, and not duplicate effort. Every local police department would use the county jail for prisoners kept overnight. It only made sense.

So all he had to do was wait for a sheriff's van. There could be no other reason to have it at the police department. When he saw it, he would then neutralize it.

Then the Sandip problem would be laid to rest for good. And Sandip as well.

He smiled at his own pun.

Chapter Seventeen

IT STILL FELT like working hours to Bentley, even though he was on paid administrative leave. He walked into the pizza place on San Luis, at Salinas Street, and every fiber of his being told him he should be in the squad room, finishing his reports.

Bentley ignored his fiber, as he often did.

The pizza place in question made a decent pie, but could never be called by the name on the sign. Doing so would make locals remark on the time, several owners ago, when a teacher that you've never heard of, from North High, owned part of the business.

It was like a knee-jerk reaction to the name; it automatically made people remark on the teacher, even though the place had sold several times since then.

Bentley ordered a large pepperoni. It had crossed his mind to order a veggie delight, but while helping Yorga lose a few pounds would be a friendly thing to do, the effort might not be worth the antagonism.

A police cruiser shot down Salinas Street, siren wailing, and took a right on San Luis, then disappeared South on Church Street. Bentley idly wondered what was going on, but it was very much not his problem: It probably wasn't a homicide, and if it were, he wasn't allowed to take cases right then.

A large white panel truck, the bottom third decorated with spray-painted graffiti, lumbered down Salinas Street in the middle lane, making the curve onto John Street. Bentley idly wondered if all the graffiti artists were short, or if they were making a statement of some kind.

He shrugged and turned back to the pizza counter.

With the box in hand, he walked out into the parking lot on Salinas Street, behind the camera shop. A gray car, across from him, was a little too close. He started to back up when a thought crossed his mind.

There was a gray BMW parked across from him. He put the car back into park and turned off the engine. The text from Yorga had mentioned a gray BMW.

Bentley scanned the area for potential suspects, but no one seemed to be nearby. He got out of the car and walked around behind the beemer, where he could read the license.

It matched, but he didn't react, just in case someone was watching. He got into his car, backed out and pulled into the alley that ran behind the pizza place. A left on San Luis and a left on Main gave his a place to park.

Your suspect vehicle is on Salinas Street. Parking lot by the fabric store. Diagonal from the Methodist church.

Odd, replied Yorga. There was a pause, then a second text. *He's going after the guy I busted. The one in your apartment. To spring him, or...*

Probably to shoot him.

Bentley threw the car into gear, screeched the tires coming out of the parking spot, and sped down Main. At Alisal, his left was blocked by a van waiting to go straight across. The light changed to six-way pedestrian crossing, and for a moment people were all over the intersection. At last it went to green.

The van crept up, waiting for a car coming south. At last it turned, with annoying slowness, and crept along Alisal, stopping for the light at Lincoln.

Bentley used a parking space to squeeze past the van and make his right turn. He whipped onto the stub of Howard between the armory and the Alisal-facing restaurant and parked behind the Chinese buffet.

If I were a sniper, he mused. The armory stood out as the obvious answer.

The doors were locked. He made his way around the armory counter-clockwise, on the long side away from the police department. There were no broken windows, and no obvious signs of entry.

He thought about kneeling, and getting the off-duty pistol he kept in the ankle holster, but he was pretty sure that he wasn't supposed to be running around with a drawn pistol while on administrative leave.

The small fenced yard behind the armory, where parks and recreation kept a barbeque and a few items for special events, appeared to be locked. A closer look showed that the shackle was dangling from the hasp, but not pressed into the lock body.

He turned it and opened the gate, carefully leaving it ajar as a sign for Yorga. He made his way slowly past the barbeque and the accumulated signs, trying not to bump into anything. A small plastic bucket, resting on top of a five-gallon propane tank, was his downfall.

He bumped the tank with his foot, and the bucket fell off, clattering on the cement.

The van with the barred windows caught Louis' eye. It was just turning out of the Church Street police parking lot, onto Howard Street. It would turn on Lincoln, probably to the right, giving Louis a view of the driver's side. As slow as it would be going, shooting the driver was out of the question. It wouldn't cause a fatal crash, and it would alert Sandip.

Ideally, Sandip would be sitting at the window, just behind the driver. The bars and the metal mesh on the windows would make it impossible to tell. The windows might even be tinted.

He would need to draw them out.

As the van stopped at the intersection, Louis popped up from behind the parapet, levering the rifle into firing position. He quickly took aim, and pulled back on the trigger. As he did, the sound of a plastic bucket clattering on cement distracted him for a moment.

The shot was still mostly where he intended. As the rifle kicked against his right shoulder, the bullet, with the same energy, tore through the grill of the van. A cloud of steam erupted from the radiator.

The driver felt the impact through the frame of the van and heard the shot at the same instant. His eye immediately went to the armory roof, where a man with a rifle stood, firing at him.

The driver threw the van into reverse and punched the gas pedal. A second bullet slammed into the van, this one slicing between the radiator and the hood, shattering the water pump and the intake manifold. The engine made a clattering noise and died, leaving the van rolling slowly backwards.

The driver popped open his door and stood behind it, reaching for the pistol he would normally carry. He was new to corrections, and had forgotten that transporting prisoners was an unarmed duty.

The man on top of the armory would have been hard to shoot with a pistol, anyway. He dove back into the van, staying low and grabbing the radio. He peeked over the dash then flattened himself on the floorbed.

The gunshots were heard inside the police station. A couple of the junior officers ran to the glass doors at the front, unwisely exposing themselves, then ducked back as they discovered their folly. The experienced officers went out the back and out the far end, circling around in search of a vantage point.

Louis' hope was that the guards, out of concern for the lives of the prisoners, would open the van and let them try to take cover. In that case, picking off Sandip would be easy. He had a clear view of the back of the old post office, where the prisoners would try to hide.

His third shot went through the windshield, shattering it and filling the van with fine powdered glass. The bullet clanged against the expanded-metal barrier, then punched through the exit door at the back of the van. It was a message: Your prisoners are in danger!

A police officer with a shotgun came around the end of the police building, and fired off three quick shots towards Louis. The double-ought shot had no hope of reaching up to him. The best shot of the three shattered second-floor windows below him.

Louis ignored it and took another shot through the windshield. If the guards wouldn't open the van, maybe he would get lucky and hit Sandip anyway.

When the bucket clattered, Bentley froze. He looked up, expecting to see a rifle swing over the edge of the roof. When he heard the first shot, he ran for the ladder.

It ended about ten feet off the ground, but a good leap, assisted by a step onto a propane tank, allowed him to grad the lowest rung and swing into the building. His legs slammed against the concrete wall.

On the return swing, he raised his right arm and grabbed the next rung, and then pulled himself up, hand over hand, until he could get his feet onto the ladder.

He was vulnerable. If the sniper started shooting down the ladder, Bentley had nowhere to dodge. He was a sitting duck. For that matter, if the sniper dropped something heavy down the ladder, Bentley was dead.

But nothing came down, so Bentley kept climbing.

At the top, he stopped. He ducked down, crouching on the ladder just below the parapet edge. With his right hand, he reached down to his ankle holster. He wouldn't need to vault over the wall: He should be able to get a good shot at the sniper from the ladder itself.

The front sight of the pistol hung on the ankle-holster, pulling the gun out of his grip. He watched as it tumbled down into the small yard behind the firehouse and landed on the plastic cover of a dumpster before bouncing off and falling behind it.

He peeked over the wall. The sniper was at the far end, firing a huge rifle down towards the street. Going over the wall was suicide. Climbing down to recover his gun would take too long.

Bentley was stuck.

Jones came around the end of the police building by the rotunda. An officer was looking around the corner of the building, holding a rifle in the general direction of the sniper. Jones took the rifle from his hand.

It had been a while since he had trained at the range with long arms, but old habits die hard. His glasses wouldn't let him see the sights and the target in sharp focus at the same time, so he concentrated on his sight picture, with the furry blob at the end as the target. He raised the front sight slightly above the blob, and squeezed the trigger three times.

The .223 kicked slightly against his shoulder, three times. He lowered the muzzle to see where he had hit. Chips came off the face of the building, just a few inches below Louis' position.

Jones handed the rifle back to the uniform.

"Shoot a little high, slightly left, and fire for effect." He turned to a sergeant who was running up behind him. "What's the status on road closures?"

"Alisal is blocked from Capitol east, and same from Monterey on the other side. Same with San Luis. And Gabilan. No cars allowed south of Center Street. We're evacuating businesses, now."

"Good," said Jones, as the uniformed popped off three quick shots at Louis. "As soon as the buildings on Salinas and Alisal are clear, let this guy have everything we've got." He turned to another sergeant. "Where's the armor?"

"Our one armored rig was already moved over to the new East Alisal Street station. We're getting it gassed and on the way, right now."

"Who ordered it moved to the new building?"

"Well, there was no place to park it here."

Jones took a deep breath. It couldn't be helped. With the new building coming online next month, this sort of thing was to be expected. But the timing was horrible.

"What can we do to give them cover?"

"I've got snipers moving up onto the old post office, and we're trying to get someone onto the armory roof, but there's no cover. They'd be sitting ducks, unless we can lob some flash-bangs or something."

"Get some smoke – no, it'll blow back at us." Jones shook his head. Yeah, get some people around the back of the old firehouse with some flash-bangs. We'll keep him busy on this end of the building, so he doesn't have a chance to drop things on them."

The uniform to Jones' right got two lucky shots, sending chips of concrete off of the edge of the parapet. One of the chips caught Louis in the cheekbone, giving him a small gash. He dropped behind the wall.

Louis dropped the SMLE. The barrel was hot, affecting his accuracy. The magazine was empty; all ten rounds, plus the one in the chamber, had been plowed through the van. With luck, he caught Sandip with one of them, possibly fatally.

If not, he had made clear to Sandip that silence was golden, and that talking would be bad for his health. Crouching to stay below the line of sight, Louis ran for the other end of the armory.

He wiped his cheekbone with his hand and got blood. Annoying, but he'd live. It also meant he couldn't casually stroll back to his car. Something to deal with once he was safely away.

His plan was to jump off the end of the parapet, landing and rolling on the old Spanish-style building that was back-to-back with the old firehouse. From there, he could jump down onto the plastic lid of the dumpster behind the firehouse, and make his way east to elude the police. With luck, there would be holes in their perimeter, and he could blend in with the civilians. Once he washed his face, of course.

He set his foot onto the edge of the wall and exploded over it, just as something slammed into him from below and to the right. The weight carried him down, spinning him off course.

The plastic lid of the dumpster collapsed under the combined weight of Louis and Bentley, crushing the cardboard boxes inside as they slammed through the lid.

Bentley was up first. He didn't know if Louis was still armed, but he knew where his gun was, and he was going to need it. He rolled out of the metal box, grabbed the gun from under the dumpster, and stood up. The tiny yard spun around, and Bentley went down in a heap.

The officers, the group tasked to scale the armory roof and take down the sniper, stormed into the tiny yard. They called in an ambulance for Bentley at once. Most of them went up the ladder, while the rest secured the area below. It took them a few more minutes to spot the second unconscious man in the dumpster.

Chapter Eighteen.

AS THE SAYING goes, no job is done without a few forests of paperwork. Jones was still at his desk at nine, trying to explain how an officer on administrative leave could be found unconscious next to a sniper who had just chewed up a prisoner transport.

Between unimaginative forms that did not allow him to elucidate, and freestyle reports that required careful crafting and wordplay, he walked a delicate balance between clarity and obfuscation. It was a relief when someone knocked on the office door frame.

"Um, Ell-tee?" asked Calucci.

"Yes, Calucci," he said, waving her inside. "Please close the door."

As she closed the door, it dawned on her that he hadn't called her Socks this time. It was inevitable that people would call her that – it was the literal translation of her Corsican last name – but it was tolerable when the brass did it. It was a signal that she was one of the team.

Did this mean she wasn't one of the team anymore?

"Um, so, Ell-tee, I sorta got a tiger by the tail here. I gotta let go, but I know I'm gonna get bit."

Jones smiled, and forgot about his paperwork. "Pardon me for one moment, Socks. Have a seat."

As she slid into a chair, He picked up his cell phone and hit a speed dial number.

"Time for you to go to periscope depth," he said to the person who answered. "Drop everything. My office, five minutes."

He turned back to Calucci. "I'm going to have a second officer drop in to hear what you have to say. You know, just so that I don't make a mistake writing it down or anything. He should be here in a moment.

"Meanwhile, just make yourself comfortable. I'm just gonna sign a couple of reports here."

Comfortable was the wrong word to describe how Calucci was feeling. She had an urge to jump up and run, but if she did, she'd have two groups of people chasing her. Of the two groups, Jones, and the police, scared her the least.

The phone in her pocket started vibrating. She glanced at Jones, who was engrossed in paperwork. She pulled out the phone and looked at it. She didn't know the number. She stuck the phone back into her pocket.

There was a soft knock at the door, and a man slipped through, opening the door barely enough. He took a seat. Unfortunately for Calucci, that placed him between her and the door.

The hair and mustache screamed that he was a cop, but otherwise, he seemed as average as possible. He wore khaki slacks, an open-necked plaid button-down shirt, and a corduroy suit jacket. Calucci's job, among other things, involved being able to describe people, and she had gone through a course on identifying characteristics.

Despite that, she was fairly certain that she would not be able to pick the newcomer out of a line-up. If she tried having an artist sketch him, all she'd be able to say about him was that he was average. He didn't seem to have a single distinguishing feature, and it was almost as if he had planned it that way.

"Calucci," said Jones, "This is my friend, special agent James Reed, of the FBI. He's doing some research that I think will pertain to what you have to say."

He turned his head towards special agent Reed. "This is Officer Tina Calucci. She's in charge of our evidence room, and she just came in and asked to have a word with me about a tiger."

Reed nodded, pulled a small digital recorder out of his pocket, and said the date and time. Then he laid it in an unobtrusive spot on Jones' desk. "Just a formality," he said, casually nodding towards it.

"So," he continued, in a smooth, friendly voice. "Officer Tina Calucci, it's very nice to meet you. Now, between you, me, and Lieutenant Jones here, what's going on? Now, before you say anything, just another formality, I do have to just mention a couple of your rights…"

As he read her rights, she panicked slightly. She had hoped it wouldn't turn into that kind of interview quite so fast. But she was committed and there was no other way out of this mess. Besides, Reed seemed like a nice guy.

Yorga flashed his badge at the desk, and was allowed into the ICU without a second look. The officer on a chair, by the sliding door to Bentley's room, was a rookie that he didn't know. Yorga took it on faith that it was mutual, and the rookie didn't know him, either. Yorga nodded and held out his hand.

He accepted a clipboard from the officer, scribbled his name and badge number on it, and nodded towards the sleeping man through the glass door. "Has he been awake? Said anything?"

"No, got a bad concussion, maybe a couple of ribs broken. Not bad, but they gotta watch and see." The officer glanced side to side. "I heard he tackled the sniper, took him off the roof. Thirty feet down."

"Yeah," said Yorga. "Lucky about the dumpster fulla boxes. What about the other guy?" He hooked a thumb towards the far side of the ICU, where another cop sat on another folding chair.

"That guy? Word is, they operated on him. Knocked out in the fall, and he's banged up worse than Bentley. They got his head wrapped up."

"Alright, listen, this guy wakes up, you tell him his partner was here."

"Sure. Hey, um… What happened downtown? I only heard bits and pieces."

"Bits and pieces is all anybody knows right now. Thing to remember is this." Yorga hooked a thumb at Bentley. "This is the hero. The other guy's a felon. Keep that straight, and you know all you gotta know."

He walked out of the ICU, nodding to the other officer as he went by.

Yoshi's phone rang. It wasn't the normal number for Louis. He let it ring two more times before answering it. "Yo," he said, as a combination of name and greeting.

"Where's Sandip?"

"Who is this?"

"This is Ron Caliburn. Where's Sandip?"

Yoshi thought he had heard Louis mention Ron Caliburn, or a name something like that. It was a name that carried some weight.

"Um, he's, uh, he's in custody. At the Salinas police station. They were trying to get a statement from him."

"He'd better be airtight. Where's Louis?"

Yoshi was in an unmarked police car, sitting outside the house that Calucci shared with her sister. He had hoped for a chance to have a word with her, and persuade her to help lose the evidence on Sandip.

The question from Caliburn alarmed Yoshi more than the idea of speaking to Louis' boss. If Caliburn didn't know where Louis was, it was all breaking loose.

"Um, I can try to find out," he said.

"Don't try, Yoshi. Find out." The line went dead.

Yoshi swallowed hard. Sandip was in custody, Louis was missing. He'd better get back to the station and get things under control. He'd call Chuck, up in Santa Clara. He didn't like the guy, but maybe Chuck would know where Louis was hiding.

Chuck's number rang busy.

Yoshi threw his car into gear and headed for the station. He whipped onto Lincoln, from Market, and came to a stop. There was yellow tape stretched across the road at Central. He rolled up to the intersection, where a black and white SUV sat in the road, lights flashing.

He rolled down the window and flashed his badge at the officer, who walked over to his window.

"Hey, what's going on?"

"Yeah, we got CSU cleaning up, still. You didn't get the radio call?"

"I was interviewing a suspect, had the radio off," said the uniform. "Sniper up on the armory took out the transport to county jail."

"Anyone hurt?"

"Just the sniper, and a detective who took him out. No names on the radio yet."

"Anything on the sniper?"

"White Asian male, early forties. He's over in ICU at memorial." The uniform looked around. "I heard they're setting up a temporary command post over at the new station, on East Alisal. If I was you, I'd check in over there. These guys are gonna be cleaning this up for a few more hours."

Yoshi blanched. He didn't know much about Ron Caliburn, aside from the name. But he knew that Caliburn was not going to like this.

Chapter Nineteen

THE MOTEL, A TINY place on John Street, had last been renovated when John and Abbott Streets had been the intersection of highways 68 and 101. Now, it sat in a state of disrepair. Most of the rooms were taken up by weekly and monthly residents; folks who couldn't get a lease on an apartment. The chief advantages to the motel were that it was less expensive than other housing, and that it accepted cash.

In one of the less-broken rooms, three men stood, staring at each other. None seemed to want to be the first to speak. At last, the man who had rented the room broke the silence.

"So neither of you knows where Louis is?"

"Um, I wasn't able to confirm," said Yoshi, "But he might be in the ICU."

"How might he have gotten there?"

"So, um, look, he didn't tell anyone he was gonna—"

"How. Did. He. Get. Into the hospital!"

"He fell off a high roof. He was up on the armory shooting at the police station."

"Why?"

"I think he was trying to kill Sandip."

The man – whose real name was definitely not Ron Caliburn – scowled at Yoshi.

"It makes sense," said Chuck. "Sandip's in custody, and there's no way to get him out. They got fingerprints back from the thing in Washington, at that hotel. So he's a liability. Louis had to take him out."

"Did he succeed?"

"I don't think so," said Yoshi. "I only heard about two going to the hospital, Bentley and Louis."

"Okay, now we've got two major liabilities. There's Sandip, and there's Louis. Either one opens his mouth, boom. We're all dead."

"What are we gonna do?" asked Chuck.

"Sandip's gonna be the tougher one. Do we know where he's being held?"

"They're still trying to interrogate him," said Yoshi. "He's at the new place. They smuggled him over there even before Louis did his thing at the old police station."

"Do we know anything useful about the new building layout? Where he's being held?"

"I can get in," said Yoshi. "I'm on the task force, so nobody asks questions about where I go. I could maybe, um, finish the job."

"How come Louis didn't use you instead of trying his own little scheme?

"I guess he felt like it needed a personal touch. Him and Sandip go way back."

"Or…" Caliburn didn't complete the thought. *Or he didn't trust you. He wanted to get it done right, so he tried to do it himself.* He had a bad feeling about Yoshi. He really did not want to put the fate of this operation into the hands of a police rookie. Still, what choice did he have? He'd need Chuck over at the hospital.

"Alright," he said, at last. "Yoshi, you go over and take out Sandip. Do it right. And if you mess this up – It's gonna go a lot better for the cops to take you out than for me to find you."

He tilted his head towards the door, and Yoshi took that as a hint to leave. He didn't mind the rudeness. He was glad to be out of that little room.

Osaka was starting to sound like a good idea. He could be in San Jose in an hour, catch a Pan-Pac Express, and land in Osaka at about this time – well, he'd lose a day, so two days from now.

A long time to spend scrunched up in economy, which was probably what he could afford. But he'd be alive, and Caliburn couldn't reach him. He thought about it for almost ten minutes this time.

Then he started the car, and headed for the new police headquarters on East Alisal. He'd head for Osaka if he failed. He wouldn't give Caliburn a chance to get him.

"Got the plans?" asked Caliburn, as soon as Yoshi had closed the door. Chuck nodded, produced a large roll of blueprints, and threw them on the bed. The papers unrolled, the corners curling.

"Which page?" asked Caliburn.

"Sheet 17, the auxiliary fluid control systems."

Caliburn flipped the page open, flinging the llower numbered page to his left. They hung off the edge of the bed, and tried to pull the whole roll over onto the floor. Chuck got a hand on the stack, near the binding, just in time to stop the slide.

"What am I looking at here?"

"The ICU, here – this is the northwest corner of the building – it's got a circular counter and a kind of a bull pen area. Every nurse, every doctor in the bull pen can see every glass door all the time. They got these sliding doors where the patients are, like on the patio of a house."

"Right, with you so far."

"Bentley is here. You go after him. I go over here and take care of Louis."

"And the nurses and everybody, they just ignore us."

"So, the system I marked in blue – That's the oxygen system. There's a tap at every ICU station. This is from the 2012 remodel. They were going to close off the system, because it's preferred now to use bottled oh-two." Chuck shrugged. "Less fire risk, or that's what they claim. There was an issue back then with the back-flow devices."

"So they don't have these anymore."

"No, they do. It woulda cost too much to rip out the lines. So they abandoned them."

"Still full of oxygen?"

"No, no, they purged the lines a long time ago."

"So how does it help us?"

"Well, we bring in our own oxygen, and we push it through the lines. Last time I was in there, scoping it out, I opened a few of the valves in the unused rooms. They're not used anymore, so nobody's gonna notice. We just hook it up, and away we go."

"And then a spark, and boom, it all blows up."

"Um, not exactly. Oxygen's not really explosive. It just makes other things more explosive." Chuck tapped another set of lines, these highlighted in green. "When they built this ICU, that woulda been '96 or so, the standard was to have redundant systems. So there's another set of pipes in the wall."

Caliburn raised an eyebrow.

"We hook up oxygen on one, and argon on the other. Then we make a spark, and boom."

"Argon."

"Well, argon di-oxide. You can make it pretty easily from an over-the-counter drain cleaner and a certain type of pool treatment tablet. I've got both chemicals out in the van right now."

"Won't they notice something wrong?"

"Nah. It's colorless and odorless. But it's lighter than air, so it makes voices sound high-pitched. Like breathing from a balloon."

"How does the plan work?"

"We put on scrubs, and we walk in. I'm carrying a clipboard and following you. You stop in a couple of ordinary rooms, then you go into Bentley's room. You stick a needle into his chest and push 200 milligrams of epinephrine. He'll have a heart attack."

"They'll find needle marks on his chest in the autopsy. They'll know he was murdered."

"Not after the ICU explodes," said Chuck. "While they're doing the code blue on Bentley, it'll distract the guard on Louis. I had Yoshi check him out. A real rookie; he'll never see us coming."

"Same thing for Louis?"

"Yup. And this whole time, we're feeding in the oxygen and the gas. As we walk out of the ICU, we throw in a flash-bang. That'll give us seven seconds to take cover, because the entire end of the hospital's coming off. We don't want to be part of it."

"You sure it's safe?"

"Blowing up a building is never safe. But the strongest part of the building is the elevator shaft. With a quick dash from here to here, we're in the elevator. Boom, seismic trip, we wait for the firemen to let us out, and we evacuate with everyone else."

"You are one cold-blooded IT guy."

"Hey," said Chuck, "A man's gotta do what a man's gotta do, right?"

Yoshi touched his new proximity card to the card reader. The magnetic lock released with a loud thunk. He pushed the door open and let himself into the gleaming hallway. The walls were white. So were the ceiling tiles and the floor tiles. The only color came from the red fire alarm pull-stations.

He didn't see anyone. Maybe most folks were still over at the old place. Socks had said that moving evidence would start on the day after tomorrow. So maybe it was still a skeleton crew here. That'd make it easier to get into the holding cells and deal with Sandip.

He passed by a meeting room, with a large window into the hallway. Too late, he realized that it was full of detectives. The door popped open.

"Yoshi, just in time," said Jones. "We're getting the task force together for updates. Come on in."

Well, it couldn't be helped. He had to maintain his cover, just for one more task. He slipped through the doorway as Jones held the door for him.

"Yoshi," said Yorga. "I don't think we've ever met. I'm Detective Sergeant Franz Yorga." He held out a huge hand, and Yoshi, not knowing what else to do, took it.

"Um, shouldn't you be under arrest?"

"Nah," said Yorga, catching Yoshi's elbow with his left hand. "Warrant got quashed, and I got reinstated."

Yoshi tried to pull his hand away, but Yorga wasn't letting go. Jones, behind Yoshi, slid Yoshi's gun out of its holster. One of the other detectives caught his left elbow and held it tightly.

"Yoshi Kojiro," said Yorga. "You're under arrest for perjury under section 118, false imprisonment under section 236, and offering false evidence under section 132 of the California Penal Code. We'll probably add some more charges once the DA gets done cataloging all the counts, but those will do for now."

"What the hell!"

"You have the right to remain silent," said Jones. "Anything you say may be used against you. You can also have a designated police representative present for all proceedings from this point, in addition to your right to have an attorney present. If you cannot afford an attorney, one will be appointed for you without charge."

Yorga was tempted to add attempted murder to the list of charges, because if looks could kill, Yorga would be lying on his back, holding a lily.

"As much fun as this party is turning into," said Yorga, "I've got people I need to go see."

Chuck's immense blue scrubs, and his collection of official-looking prox cards, allowed him to roll the gas canister into the enclosed engineering area behind the hospital without any questions.

The engineering area, located midway between the emergency room and the new parking structure, was enclosed by a chain link fence. Wooden slats, inserted through the wires of the fence, partially obscured what lay beyond. Canvas covers wired to the inside of the fence completed the obfuscation.

Caliburn sat in the van, watching the fence. After several minutes, Chuck emerged again and came back to get the second tank.

The second tank took longer. Chuck poured in something powdery out of a white plastic jar. When he was done, put on rubber gloves and removed a black plastic bottle from a clear plastic bag. He leaned away from the tank as he poured in the second chemical.

As soon as the bottle was empty, he thrust it back into the plastic bag and slammed the lid onto the tank. It was no bigger than a 5-gallon cooler, the kind people take on camping trips. Somehow, the fact that a thing so small could generate so much explosive force – enough, Chuck had said, to blow the whole end off of the building – left Caliburn in awe.

Chuck wrestled it out of the van and got it strapped onto his hand truck. Then he rolled it into the engineering enclosure, where he had been before. He disappeared behind the fence.

Caliburn started the ignition, put the van into gear, and sat, idling, just in case Chuck went up in a big fireball. He could abort the mission at a moment's notice.

Chuck came back out, without even the hand truck. Caliburn hated to leave it behind. It was evidence, in the very unlikely event that someone figured out what had happened. Still, it was only a handtruck.

Chuck moved as fast as he could. He was very overweight, so that wasn't very fast. It seemed to Caliburn that it took forever for Chuck to reach the van.

Caliburn calmly drove them around to Wilgart Street, behind the parking garage. He parked at the curb, wheels turned out, towards Romie Lane.

"Let's go through the plan," said Chuck. "We're both in scubs, both with clipboards. There's a guard outside Bentley's room. You walk past him, stick the needle, escape in the code. I slip past the other guard and take out

Louis. One, two, we meet by the door, three, throw a flashbang, and four, run."

"Why don't you stand overwatch, and keep an eye to make sure no one's too nosy? Or hold the staff at gunpoint while I take out our targets?"

"I've wanted to shoot Louis for a long time. Please give me the pleasure."

Caliburn nodded. "Knock yourself out. How do we know if the gas is taking effect?"

"Their voices will be squeaky. The gas is lighter than air. It'll be obvious."

"So after we're both back at the front door to the ICU, then we throw the Flash-bang and run."

"Right. The elevator is second right, then left. Remember that. Second right, then left. We just need to be near the doors of it. So long as the shaft is between us and the explosion, we should be fine. "

"You got the needles?"

Chuck passed him a hypodermic syringe and a small suppressed .22 LR pistol. "Just in case," he said. "Loaded, safety on, one in the chamber."

"Cocked and locked," said Caliburn.

"Bingo. Don't forget to take the cap off the needle before you stick him." Chuck lifted a second needle, held it to the light, and slipped it into the left pocket of his scrubs. He placed a pistol into the right pocket.

"Lights, camera," said Chuck.

"Action." The men got out of the van and walked towards the ICU.

The Ford Crown Victorias screamed down South Main, lights flashing and sirens screaming. As they cut around the corner onto Romie Lane, the lead car cut its siren. The others followed suit, and from Pajaro street on, they relied on the lights to get traffic out of the way.

Two cars dashed to the corner of Los Palos and blocked it diagonally, forcing traffic onto Romie, towards Abbott. Two more whipped around the corner, racing to block traffic at Los Palos and San Jose streets.

Yorga, with Jones in the passenger seat, followed two cars down Wilgart. They screeched to a stop in the middle of the road, as the cruisers raced ahead to the intersection.

"That's the van," said Special Agent Reed, from the back seat. "They're in the ICU."

"Should we evacuate the area?" asked Jones, as the three men scrambled out of the car.

"No need," said Reed, dashing towards the entrance. "We've got it contained."

They dashed across the small lobby, and hooked left, along a glass-enclosed walkway. The signs pointed left, and Special Agent Reed shouldered his way through the door, bringing up his pistol as he did.

"Hey," came an unnaturally squeaky voice. "You can't bring those in here!" A woman in pink scrubs stood behind the counter, her eyes huge. Reed flashed his badge and signaled for her to duck.

An alarm sounded in Bentley's nook; a squealing beep, demanding immediate attention. It was followed by the crash of something tipping over. There was a clatter of articles bouncing off of the terrazzo floor.

Jones and Yorga got there at the same instant, pointing their guns at the figure on the floor. "Freeze," they both yelled, but Bentley was already standing with one foot on the suspect's back. His service pistol was in his hand, pointed at Caliburn's head. A hypodermic needle dangled from his chest.

Jones reached over to the monitor and silenced the alarm. "Looks like you got this one," he said. He held his own gun on the suspect while Yorga handcuffed Caliburn.

Bentley sat back down on the bed. "That's a lot of exercise for a man who's been in bed for three days. I need a rest."

"Thought he had you for a second," said Yorga. "The alarms threw me."

"Leads pulled loose when I threw him on the floor." He looked around. "Hey, there was a second guy with him! I think he went for the suspect!"

Just then, Chuck appeared in the doorway. Bentley brought his gun arm up, but Special Agent Reed knocked it out of the way. "He's with me," said Reed.

In the confusion, Caliburn reached into his pocket and produced a flash-bang grenade. He yanked the pin and flung it towards the bull pen.

Yorga tried to catch it, but only deflected it. It clattered against the edge of the doorway, then bounced around the little glass nook, ending up under the bed.

"You were supposed to ..." shouted Reed at Chuck, just as the grenade went off.

There was a brilliant flash. Even from under the bed, it was blinding, and the concussion was deafening. Caliburn, on the floor beside the bed, took the brunt of it, screaming from the aural pain.

Bentley felt the bed move slightly, then opened his eyes and uncovered his ears.

Jones staggered around the foot of the bed. He had managed to close his eyes, but his gun had kept him from covering his right ear. He felt like he was on a boat, and that it was tilting randomly.

Yorga was sprawled beside the bed, arm over the top of his head, left forefinger stuffed into his right ear. He said a bad word and opened his eyes. Caliburn was writhing on the floor, so Yorga sat on him.

Agent Reed was holding the foot of the bed and shaking his head. He had somehow avoided the effects of the intense noise, but his ears clearly hurt, nonetheless. He carefully reached up and removed earplugs from his ears.

Chuck, and the supposed nurse at the front counter, had fared best. Both had been outside the nook, out of the direct line of sight, and the smoke just before the explosion was enough to make them cover their ears.

Chuck poked his head around the corner. "Everyone okay in here?"

Jones shook his head. The ringing in his ears was still there, but the seasickness was already waning. The others each held up a thumb.

"You were supposed to have the flash-bang, not him," shouted Reed. "And it was supposed to be a dud."

"I've got it here," said Chuck. "Guess he had a spare, just in case."

"Chuck, why didn't we just blow up right now?" yelled Caliburn. "I heard the nurse's squeaky voice and everything."

"Meet policewoman Tina Calucci," said Jones, in a voice far too loud for the circumstances. "She took a breath from a helium balloon."

"Calucci? From the evidence…" he cut himself off just before shouting an incriminating utterance, but it was obvious what he was about to say. Frustration dominated his face.

"Yup," said Jones. "We turned her. She'll do some jail time, but the DA will consider her cooperation here today. Going into harm's way, that sort of thing."

"Goes with the badge," she said. Then her face changed, as she realized that, effective immediately, she no longer had a badge, and never would again.

Bentley looked down and saw the hypodermic needle dangling from his chest. He hadn't felt it when it went in, and barely did, even now.

The plunger was all the way down. "Hey, fellas, should I be worried about this?" he asked.

Epilogue:

THE SMALL BOAT rocked on the twilight waters of San Diego harbor. Shelter Island, to the north of the boat, and North Island, to the south, each offered strings of sparkling lights, all along the shore.

Neither island was a true island, but no one on the boat felt like splitting hairs over it. It could be claimed that they were fishing, and they even had licenses, but none of the lines dangling in the water actually had bait, or even a hook.

Earl Licowicz reached into the cooler and brought out another beer. He offered one to Yorga and to Bentley, but both just shook their heads.

"Okay, I still don't get it," he said. With the sun setting off Point Loma, he no longer needed the dark sunglasses, so he raised them onto the top of his head. They left a white pattern across his eyes, like a reverse raccoon mask.

Yorga shrugged. "Okay, so me and Bentley went up to that food festival in Washington, right? Well, we had a funny feeling about that place."

Bentley, relaxing on the chair to Yorga's right, didn't bother opening his eyes. "Wasn't our jurisdiction. None of our business."

"Man's got enough trouble one day at a time," said Earl. "So they were doing what?"

"They were the money. Ships coming south along the coast, money would arrive in crates at Astoria, and wind up at the hotel. Mostly through that one dry cleaner, but they had a couple of tricks for getting it up there to the island," said Yorga.

"Hotel deposits the money, puts it on their books, makes up expenses against it, and spits it out, clean as a whistle," said Bentley.

"I never seen a clean whistle," said Earl. "I was always worried about usin' 'em. Who knew where the last guy's mouth had been?"

"Anyway," said Yorga, "The hotel was laundering the money. They made it all look legit."

"You guys took them down?"

"Nah, we just happened to be up there. Took care of a murder case for the sheriff, but we missed the money."

"We weren't looking for it. We knew something was dodgy, but it wasn't our problem," insisted Bentley.

"Langer, Sheriff Langer, one of his guys wound up taking down the money. But that's a different story."

"Okay, so get back to this one," said Earl. What was the deal with the guns?"

"Alright, so they had a safe house in Chualar. Figured nobody's gonna look for a contraband warehouse like that in a tiny little town."

"With you so far."

"Corrupt cops – they were turning cops all over the state. Not lots, just one or two, here or there. People with access to evidence lockups. Guns come in, they get used for evidence, if the owner can't be found, the guns get destroyed. That's what's supposed to happen.

"But these guys were slippin' them out the back door. Collect 'em up in Santa Clara to sort 'em and price 'em – lots of different kinds of freight going through there, lots of available warehouses. Easy to shuffle the deck."

"Took a cruise one time where they had that shuffle-deck thing, but I didn't get it. Every time I was up – oh, you meant like cards."

"Yeah. They could move offices easy."

"How'd they get 'em to Chualar?"

"Train. Freight goes by Chualar all the time, and there's a kind of a kink in the tracks right there. You gotta slow down to around thirty for a few miles."

"Just the one the freight trains use. Not the main line. The one for the Coast Starlight is fine," said Bently.

"So they're slowed, so what?" asked Earl.

"This group, this Caliburn guy—"

"Rothenberg," corrected Bentley. "It was that Leon Rothenberg, one of the managers at that hotel. He was up there pretending to run a hotel for years, but it was all about laundering the money."

"Right, right," said Earl. "What about the guns?"

"So they turned a guy at a freight yard," said Yorga. "He'd get them onto southbound trains, along with a guy who rode along. Passing Chualar, this guy pushed the crates off the train. They kept some dirt all plowed up next to the tracks, by the eucalyptus trees. Some guys would grab the crates, and drive 'em over to the safe house in Chualar."

"Why not just let 'em ride down to LA?"

"Because the rail yards in LA are a lot bigger. More people. Better security. More chance of someone looking at the wrong crate. More chance of getting caught."

"So they took 'em by truck instead."

"Right. Straight down to LA, and then onto a north-bound ship, inside a few specially rigged containers. They smuggled 'em into Vancouver, sold 'em in batches to an organization there, and brought the money back the same way. Dropped the cash in Astoria, and the hotel did the rest. Like clockwork."

"I dunno," said Earl. "Seems to me, one of Mickey's hands ain't on his face."

"Yeah, ain't that the truth," said Bentley.

"Anyway, between Sandip and Socks both turning state's evidence, they have enough on Rothenberg to keep him locked up till his grandkids are old and gray. If he even has any."

"Sounds like you guys done a good deed, getting' those guys off the street. Lemme buy you a beer." Earl reached into the cooler again, but the other two waved him off.

"You go ahead," said Yorga. "We're good."

Point Loma slowly faded into darkness, then lit up as the lights came on. Yorga grinned, savoring the moment. For the first time in months, he didn't have to look over his shoulder.

"Okay," said Bentley. "The little note in the pizza restaurant. The one that tipped you off."

"Oh, that," said Yorga. "That was Lieutenant Jones. He didn't confess until after it was over, of course. He's talking about retiring. Apparently that flash-bang really messed up his ear. Bad tinnitus."

"Everyone said I got a tin ear," said Earl. He tossed a beer can into a plastic bucket and slid his hand into the cooler for another. "Never heard of tin-itis. And it never stopped me."

"Go easy on that stuff," said Bentley. "You've gotta get us back to shore later."

"No worry," said Earl. He cracked open the beer can. "Of course, that needle I got stuck with—"

"Saline solution. Just salt water. Chuck didn't want you dead, of course," said Yorga. "We knew that."

"Okay, that's another thing," said Earl. "The bad guy stuck you with the needle, but the guy who gave it to him was what, an undercover?"

"Special Agent Chuck Fowlgarten," said Bentley.

"Layers on layers," said Yorga. "There was the Task Force, that Bentley and Kojiro were on. Mostly people that they thought were bent, plus Bentley to keep 'em straight. And to report back."

"That who thought was bent?" asked Earl.

"The real task force. Jones, Agent Reed, and our buddy Chuck. Seems Special Agent Fowlgarten spent a couple of years working his way into Louis' team. Nearly panicked when me and Bentley solved those murders up at the hotel."

"Then panicked for real when Langer blew that hotel thing wide open," said Bentley.

"They thought they'd lost Rothenberg, but they played it slow, gave him a little rope, and next thing you know, he's back in business. Different laundry."

"So you guys said something about that gun Herb tried a melt," said Earl. "It had some kinda fishing weight in it, but wouldn't melt?"

"Yup," said Bentley. "Tungsten. They make fishing weights out of it, not toxic like lead. Density is the same as gold, but it's a lot cheaper, and you can't melt it with acetylene. You need something hotter."

"So these guys Kojiro was workin' with, they made a gun outta fishing weights?"

"No, They 3D-printed the general shape of the barrel and the two receivers — the parts that make up the gun itself. The parts hardest to replace. Then they stuffed the plastic pieces full of tungsten bits to make up the weight."

"Must've thought Herb would crush it in a press or something," said Yorga. "But he hits it with the acetylene, and gets a fire."

"The Lahti's still out there somewhere," said Bentley. "Wonder if it ever made its way back to that crew outta Redding. The hit team with the one-time pads."

"I think they got closed down," said Yorga. "Feds were all over 'em."

"Yeah, too deep for me," said Earl, guzzling the last of the beer and tossing the empty can into the bucket.

He looked across the dark waters. A flight of F-22s, just visible by their running lights and afterburner flames, took off from North Island, screaming off into the night.

"You guys ready to head in?" he asked. "There's a coffee shop I eat at sometimes, down in Chula Vista. They got a whirly-bird special. Stupid name for it, but if you get there by five, it's half-price."

"Might be a bit late for that," said Yorga.

"We could still eat," said Earl.

Bentley and Yorga shrugged at each other.

"Might as well," said Yorga.

www.ingramcontent.com/pod-product-compliance
Lightning Source LLC
Chambersburg PA
CBHW020643260626
47157CB00008B/2887